CRISPUS ATTUCKS

James Neyland

MELROSE SQUARE PUBLISHING COMPANY
LOS ANGELES, CALIFORNIA

JAMES NEYLAND is the author of four other biographies in Melrose Square's Black American Series—*George Washington Carver, Booker T. Washington, W.E.B. Du Bois,* and *A. Philip Randolph*—as well as two novels published by Holloway House, *The Fever* and *The Dark Lady*.

*To Thomas Danisi,
historian, poet, and friend.*

Consulting Editor for Melrose Square
Raymond Friday Locke

Originally published by Melrose Square, Los Angeles.
© 1995 by Holloway House.

Cover Painting by Jesse Santos
Cover Design by Bill Skurski

CRISPUS ATTUCKS

MELROSE SQUARE
BLACK AMERICAN SERIES

ELLA FITZGERALD
singer
NAT TURNER
slave revolt leader
PAUL ROBESON
singer and actor
JACKIE ROBINSON
baseball great
LOUIS ARMSTRONG
musician
SCOTT JOPLIN
composer
MATTHEW HENSON
explorer
MALCOLM X
militant black leader
CHESTER HIMES
author
SOJOURNER TRUTH
antislavery activist
BILLIE HOLIDAY
singer
RICHARD WRIGHT
writer
ALTHEA GIBSON
tennis champion
JAMES BALDWIN
author
JESSE OWENS
olympics star
MARCUS GARVEY
black nationalist leader
SIDNEY POITIER
actor
WILMA RUDOLPH
track star
MUHAMMAD ALI
boxing champion
FREDERICK DOUGLASS
patriot & activist
MARTIN LUTHER KING, JR.
civil rights leader
ZORA NEALE HURSTON
author
SARAH VAUGHAN
singer
LANGSTON HUGHES
poet

HARRY BELAFONTE
singer & actor
JOE LOUIS
boxing champion
MAHALIA JACKSON
gospel singer
BOOKER T. WASHINGTON
educator
NAT KING COLE
singer & pianist
GEORGE W. CARVER
scientist & educator
WILLIE MAYS
baseball player
LENA HORNE
singer & actress
DUKE ELLINGTON
jazz musician
BARBARA JORDAN
congresswoman
GORDON PARKS
photographer & director
MADAME C.J. WALKER
entrepreneur
MARY MCLEOD BETHUNE
educator
THURGOOD MARSHALL
supreme court justice
KATHERINE DUNHAM
dancer & choreographer
ELIJAH MUHAMMAD
religious leader
ARTHUR ASHE
tennis champion
A. PHILIP RANDOLPH
union leader
W.E.B. DU BOIS
scholar & activist
DIZZY GILLESPIE
musician & bandleader
COUNT BASIE
musician & bandleader
HENRY AARON
baseball player
MEDGAR EVERS
social activist
RAY CHARLES
singer & musician

CONTENTS

CRISPUS ATTUCKS
SAMUEL MAVERICK
JAMES CALDWELL
SAMUEL GRAY
PATRICK CARR

MARCH 5, 1770

Chapter One

The First American Hero

ON WEDNESDAY, November 14, 1888, the citizens of Boston, Massachusetts, gathered on the Boston Common for the dedication of a monument to a man they knew very little about other than that he was the first man to die in the American Revolution. Of course, they knew his name—Crispus Attucks—and the fact that he was an African American, but most of the details of his life had been lost in history.

Indeed, there had been some controversy over whether or not he and the four other men who died with him in the Boston

The monument on Boston Common dedicated to Crispus Attucks and the other victims of the Boston Massacre created a considerable controversy at the time of its dedication in 1888.

Massacre were truly deserving of a monument. Some people attempted to minimize their contribution to the cause of freedom because they were not prominent men but working-class people, and Crispus Attucks himself had been a runaway slave.

It took a few determined leaders of Boston's African-American community more than twenty years to convince the city government and the state legislature to allocate the money jointly to erect the monument, the first ever to be paid for by public funds in the Commonwealth of Massachusetts. And on this day, representatives of both state and city government were present for the dedication, joining with the black community.

It was a beautiful day for a public celebration; the sky was clear and the sun was shining brightly. There was a cool, rather chilly, fall breeze wafting in from the harbor only a few blocks away. The celebration began with a parade that started off from the corner of Beacon and Charles streets at eleven o'clock in the morning, led by the Germania Band playing patriotic marches, followed by the black regiment of the Massachusetts Volunteer Militia and the carriages of the nineteen members of the Crispus Attucks Monument Committee.

The Chairman of the Committee was

William H. Dupree, who had distinguished himself as a lieutenant in the 55th Massachusetts Volunteers in the Civil War, one of the two celebrated black regiments from the state. Among the other African-American notables on the committee riding in the parade was Archibald Grimke, publisher of the Boston *Hub* and a successful author of biographies, and the elderly Lewis Hayden whose years of effort for a monument had finally led to this day.

At the State House, the governor, the lieutenant governor, and others from the state government joined the procession in their carriages. At City Hall, the carriages of the mayor and the city aldermen fell into line.

When they arrived at the Boston Common, the new monument was hidden from view behind a drapery, and a temporary wooden platform had been erected alongside it. As the band played, the notables—both whites and blacks—ascended the platform and took their places. Then Reverend Eli Smith of Springfield stepped forward and led an opening prayer, after which William H. Dupree rose to introduce Governor Oliver Ames.

Governor Ames, assisted by a child, Lillian Chapelle, daughter of J.C. Chapelle, one of the African Americans who had fought for so long to make the memorial a reality, removed

The dedication ceremonies for the Crispus Attucks monument included not only an unveiling, seen above in a drawing that appeared in the Boston Daily Globe, but also parades, speeches,

a dinner, and two parties that lasted far into the night. African-American dignitaries came to Boston from all over the country to participate in honoring the first hero of the American Revolution.

the drapery from the monument.

The crowd that had gathered in front of the podium cheered loudly. The monument's designer, Robert Kraus, smiled proudly.

The monument was impressive, consisting of a cylindrical obelisk of Concord granite rising over twenty-four feet, containing a band of thirteen stars at the top, representing the original colonies, and below them the names of the five men who died in the massacre— Crispus Attucks, Samuel Maverick, James Caldwell, Samuel Gray, and Patrick Carr.

On the front of the square base was a bronze bas relief depicting the massacre itself, with the citizens confronting the British troops in King Street (now State Street), the body of Crispus Attucks lying already dead in the foreground and the Old State House and the Old Brick Church visible in the background.

The bronze sculpture by Robert Kraus, representing the allegorical figure of "Free America," stood grandly on the base in front of the obelisk, her left hand holding a flag about to be unfurled and her right hand raised clasping the broken chain of oppression. Crushed beneath her right foot was the royal British crown; at her side was an eagle preparing to take flight.

Governor Ames officially presented the

monument to Boston on behalf of the Commonwealth of Massachusetts, and Mayor Hugh O'Brien accepted it with a gracious speech.

The ceremonies concluded with the playing of "The Star Spangled Banner," but the celebration was just beginning. The parade reformed and marched through Tremont, Court, and State streets by the site where the Boston Massacre had taken place, then proceeded in front of the Old State House to Faneuil Hall. There, the dignitaries and guests left the parade and went inside for further ceremonies, which began at one o'clock.

Inside, the Germania Band played a medley of patriotic songs, and the Reverend Albert H. Plumb began the second set of ceremonies with a prayer. Again Chairman Dupree introduced Governor Ames.

This time, the Governor gave a longer oration, saying: "We have just come from our beloved Common, where has been unveiled a monument erected to the memory of a noble race and noble men. Those men who are our special guests today are representatives of a race whose brother Attucks was the first one to fall in that great massacre. The opinions of other and wiser men have been given, and I will only say that this is a most fitting tribute to the memory of an occasion which did much toward freeing our nation from British rule."

Mayor O'Brien also spoke longer and more passionately than he had at the monument itself, saying: "I am aware that the monument to Crispus Attucks and his martyr associates has been the subject of more or less adverse criticism, and that by some they are looked upon as rioters, who deserved their fate. I look upon it from an entirely different standpoint. The Boston Massacre was one of the most important and exciting events that preceded our revolution. The throwing of the tea overboard in Boston harbor, the Boston massacre, Paul Revere's ride to Lexington, with other exciting events, had, no doubt, great influence in uniting the colonists as one man against unjust taxation and British oppression; made possible the war of the revolution, and the Declaration of Independence, that immortal document which pronounced all men free and equal without regard to color, creed, or nationality.

"I rejoice with you, Mr. Chairman, that after the lapse of more than one hundred years, the erection of the Attucks monument on Boston Common ratifies the words of that declaration, that all men are free and equal, without regard to color, creed, or nationality,

It was largely through the efforts of Lewis Hayden (top) that the monument to Crispus Attucks was erected. Archibald Grimke (bottom), as publisher of the Boston Hub, *used his influence in the campaign and served on the monument committee.*

and that the memory of the martyrs whose blood was shed in the cause of liberty in 1770 will thus be preserved and honored for all time."

There was great applause as he stepped down. However, the most moving part of the ceremonies was the reading by Reverend Andrew Chamberlin of a poem composed by John Boyle O'Reilly for the occasion:

Where shall we seek for a hero, and where shall
*   we find a story?*
Our laurels are wreathed for conquest, our songs
*   for completed glory;*
But we honor a shrine unfinished, a column
*   uncapped with pride,*
If we sing the deed that was sown like seed when
*   Crispus Attucks died.*

Shall we take for a sign this negro slave with
*   unfamiliar name—*
With his poor companions, nameless too, till their
*   lives leaped forth in flame?*
Yea, surely, the verdict is not for us to render or
*   deny;*
We can only interpret the symbol; God chose these
*   men to die—*
As teachers, perhaps, that to humble lives may
*   chief award be made;*
That from lowly ones and rejected stones, the tem-
*   ple's base is laid!*

When the bullets leaped from the British guns,

no chance decreed their aim;
Men see what the royal hirelings saw—a multi-
tude and a flame;
But beyond the flame, a mystery; five dying men
in the street,
While the streams of severed races in the will of
a nation meet!

Oh, blood of the people! changeless tide, through
century, creed, and race!
Still one as the sweet salt sea is one, though tem-
pered by sun and place;
The same in the ocean currents and the same in
the sheltered seas;
Forever the fountain of common hopes and kind-
ly sympathies;
Indian and Negro, Saxon and Celt, Teuton and
Latin and Gaul—
Mere surface shadow and sunshine, while the
sounding unifies all!
One love, one hope, one duty theirs! No matter
the time or ken,
There never was separate heart-beat in all the
races of men!

But alien is one—of class, not race—he has
drawn the time for himself:
His roots drink life from inhuman soil, from
garbage of pomp and pelf;
He times his heart from the common beat, he has
changed his life-stream's hue;
He deems his flesh to be finer flesh, he boasts that
his blood is blue;
Patrician, aristocrat, tory—whatever his age or
name,

*To the people's rights and liberties, a traitor ever
    the same;*
*The natural crowd is a mob to him, their prayer
    a vulgar rhyme;*
*The freedman's speech is sedition, and the patri-
    ot's deed a crime;*
*Wherever the race, the law, the land—whatever
    the time or throne,*
*The tory is always a traitor to every class but his
    own.*

*Thank God for a land where pride is clipped,
    where arrogance stalks apart;*
*Where law and song and loathing of wrong are
    words of the common heart;*
*Where the masses honor straightforward
    strength, and know, when veins are bled,*
*That the bluest blood is putrid blood—that the
    people's blood is red!*

*And honor to Crispus Attucks, who was leader
    and voice that day;*
*The first to defy, and the first to die, with
    Maverick, Carr, and Gray.*
*Call it riot or revolution, his hand first clenched
    at the crown;*
*His feet were the first in perilous place to pull the
    king's flag down;*
*His breast was the first one rent apart, that lib-
    erty's stream might flow;*
*For our freedom now and forever, his head was
    the first laid low.*

* * * * * *

O, Planter of seed in thought and deed! has the
year of right revolved,
And brought the negro patriot's cause with its
problem to be solved?
His blood streamed first for the building, and
through all the century's years.
Our growth of story and fame of glory are mixed
with his blood and tears.

He lived with men like a soul condemned—derid-
ed, defamed, and mute;
Debased to the brutal level, and instructed to be
a brute;
His virtue was shorn of benefit, his industry of
reward;
His love!—oh men, it were mercy to have cut
affection's cord;
Through the night of his woe, no pity save that
of his fellow slave;
For the wage of his priceless labor, the scourging
block and the grave!

And now, is the tree to blossom? Is the bowl of
agony filled?
Shall the price be paid, and the honor said, and
the word of outrage stilled?
And we who have toiled for freedom's law, have
we sought for freedom's soul?
Have we learned at last that human right is not
a part, but the whole?
That nothing is told while the clinging sin
remains part unconfessed?
That the health of the nation is periled if one man
be oppressed?

Has he learned—the slave from the rice swamps
  whose children were sold—has he,
With broken chains on his limbs, and the cry in
  his blood, "I am free!"
Has he learned through affliction's teaching what
  our Crispus Attucks knew—
When right is stricken the white and black are
  counted as one, not two?
Has he learned that his century of grief was
  worth a thousand years
In blending his life and blood with ours, and that
  all his toils and tears
Were heaped and poured on him suddenly, to give
  him a right to stand
From the gloom of African forests, in the blaze of
  the forest land?
That his hundred years have earned for him a
  place in the human van
Which others have fought for and thought for
  since the world of wrong began?

For this, shall his vengeance change to love, and
  his retribution burn,
Defending the right, the weak, and the poor, when
  each shall have his turn;
For this, shall he set his wo[e]ful past afloat on
  the stream of night;
For this, he forgets as we all forget when dark-
  ness turns to light;
For this, he forgives as we all forgive when wrong
  has changed to right.

And so must we come to the learning of Boston's
  lesson today;
The moral that Crispus Attucks taught in the old

heroic way;
God made mankind to be one in blood, as one in
*   spirit and thought;*
And so great a boon, by a brave man's death, is
*   never dearly bought!*

The celebration continued with a banquet at Parker's Hotel, which began at four in the afternoon, and two large parties that night, one hosted by the Sixth Regiment of the Massachusetts Volunteer Militia at the Odd Fellows Hall and the other by the Colored Knights of Pythias at the Ebenezer Baptist Church.

As the celebrating progressed, the speakers became more numerous and more eloquent. At the banquet, Mayor O'Brien braved controversy to say, "This event teaches us two things, equality and fellowship of the races. I am sometimes called an Irish American. I don't like it. I am not an Irish American; I am an American, through and through. In this country there are no others than Americans."

Black representatives from other states were also invited to speak at the banquet. Perhaps the most prominent of these was P.B.S. Pinchback of Louisiana, who had served the Union as Captain of the Second Louisiana Volunteers in the Civil War and had been Lieutenant Governor of Louisiana, serving briefly as acting governor during Reconstruction. In his speech he said: "I have been impressed today by the tribute paid to us; but no spectacle seems so grand as that I see before me, the ruler of the state here, of the city here, Anglo Saxons both, and your black chairman between them—perfect equality of the races."

Pinchback may have been somewhat carried away by the exuberance of the moment, for it was not, in truth, perfect equality; it was merely a public demonstration in favor of equality by some whites and some blacks in hopes of promoting a resolution of conflict between the races at a time when freedmen in some parts of the country were beginning to lose the rights they had won after the Civil War.

Even in Boston, the home of the abolition movement, the races were not unified, nor was there unity among whites and blacks themselves. At a time when the African-American citizens of Boston should have been celebrating the recognition of Crispus Attucks, it was divided in a dispute over which of its leaders had really begun the movement for a monument back in 1861—William C. Nell or Lewis Hayden.

Nell, who had died in 1874, was not being recognized in the official ceremonies, while

Among the African-American dignitaries participating in the dedication of the Crispus Attucks monument were W.H. Dupree (top), who chaired the monument committee, and P.B.S. Pinchback (bottom), former Governor of Louisiana.

the elderly—but living—Hayden was. Both men had fought long and hard for official recognition of the contribution of Crispus Attucks in American history, and it was Hayden who had finally succeeded, fourteen years after the death of Nell. Yet it seems to be a part of human nature to look for points on which to divide rather than unite.

After the banquet was over, the celebrants divided between two separate parties. The official one planned by the monument committee was hosted by Company L of the Sixth Regiment of the Massachusetts Volunteer Militia at the Odd Fellows Hall, and it was the larger of the two, with dancing to the Wright Orchestra until three o'clock in the morning. Nell's supporters chose to celebrate at a more sedate affair sponsored by the Colored Knights of Pythias at the Ebenezer Baptist Church on Springfield Street.

Curiously, after more than a hundred years, both Nell and Hayden have been virtually forgotten, yet both made major contributions to history far more important than the erection of a monument. Before the Civil War, Hayden had been a leader of the Underground Railroad, as prominent as Harriet Tubman or Sojourner Truth; and Nell had been a lawyer who was denied admission to the Massachusetts bar because he would not swear to uphold the U.S. Constitution as long as it permitted slavery, and so became assistant to Frederick Douglass and one of the first important black historians.

This minor controversy tends to affirm the truth of William Shakespeare's words in *Julius Caesar*: "The evil that men do lives after them; the good is oft interred with their bones...." However, it may be argued that this truth is entirely dependent upon who writes the history books. In the case of Crispus Attucks, popular legend portrays him as a hero—indeed, the first real American hero— yet scholarly historians frequently attempt to portray him as a villain, minimizing his contribution to history in favor of the leaders of the American Revolution, the statesmen like John Adams and Thomas Jefferson who continued to make contributions to history.

Most of the facts about the life of Crispus Attucks were buried with him in 1770, yet his place in history is of such significance that it is worth an attempt to exhume them in hopes of understanding the man.

Chapter Two

A Yankee Slave

VERY FEW PROVEN and substantiated facts have survived about the life of Crispus Attucks, the man who became the first American hero. Much of his "story" is legend or myth, and as such it has been the subject of dispute among historians, most of whom have been white supremacists attempting to deny the importance of African-American participation in the American Revolution. Some, unable to deny that Attucks performed an act of heroism, have even attempted to prove that he was not of African heritage.

Yet that is one fact that is quite clear:

The African slave trade was hardly as it is depicted in this artist's fanciful interpretation. For those who survived the horrible ordeal of the ocean voyage, the New World offered no joy.

Crispus Attucks was a mulatto, and he had been a slave. His father, Prince Attucks, was born in Africa, probably Guinea or Sierra Leone, and brought to Massachusetts as a young man in the early part of the eighteenth century. Crispus' mother, Nancy, was a "Natick" Indian, a part of the settlement of the first Native Americans to be "christianized" in New England. It is also clear that Crispus was born about 1723 among the Naticks.

It seems unlikely that he became a slave at birth, for his mother was a free woman, living with the other Christian Indians on the banks of Cochituate Lake near Natick, about fifteen miles west of Boston and less than five miles east of Framingham. However, his status was probably ambiguous from the time of his birth because of his mixed parentage. Contrary to popular belief, the Indians—especially those attempting to assimilate into the white culture—did not have a natural affinity for the African slaves. They did have family, or tribal, loyalty, and therefore Nancy and her mulatto child were probably tolerated, at least until Crispus began to mature.

In order to try to piece together the life of Crispus Attucks, it is important to understand something of the nature of the institution of slavery as it existed in New England and the rest of the North American continent. It did not begin with the importation of Africans, but with the capture and exportation of Indians to Spain and the Caribbean islands as slaves. In fact, the famed Squanto, who served as interpreter and taught the Pilgrims how to plant corn and get through the winter of 1620, spoke English because he had been one of twenty-six Patuxet and Nauset Indians captured by an English adventurer in 1614 and sold into slavery in Spain, having been freed and returned to Cape Cod in 1619 only to find that most of his tribe had been wiped out by disease in 1616, along with a great number of other Indians living along the New England coast.

This plague of smallpox and yellow fever was brought to the new land by the early explorers, though King James I of England and the Puritans thought that God in His Divine Providence had wiped out the Massachusetts tribes so that they, the Christians, could settle the area.

It was this same religious bigotry, not racism, that created the American slave system. Christians of the time, both Catholic and Protestant, believed that their religion made them superior to all other peoples, who were considered "heathens" merely because they did not subscribe to their specific religious rituals. They believed that intolerance was a virtue, and God expected them to persecute, even execute, non-Christians and Christians of other sects than their own. It was certainly acceptable for "heathens" to be sold into slavery.

For example, the famed Puritan leader Cotton Mather was so outraged by the prospect of William Penn settling a colony of Quakers in what became Pennsylvania that he seriously recommended intercepting the ship and selling the Quakers into slavery in Barbados.

The New Englanders' trading in slaves began in earnest in 1637, after the Puritans defeated the Pequot Indians and put the captured Native Americans aboard the *Desire*, which sailed from Salem, Massachusetts, for the Caribbean. Six years later, in 1643, a Boston ship, carrying rum, picked up blacks in Africa and delivered them to Barbados, exchanging them for molasses, thus starting the "triangle trade."

However, in the beginning, the colonists of Massachusetts Bay and Virginia, of New Netherlands and Carolina, did not feel a need to own slaves themselves. They had indentured servants who served their purposes, poor people from Europe who signed con-

This advertisement for the sale of slaves clearly shows that a major concern of prospective buyers was smallpox. It was an even greater problem for the slaves themselves and the seamen on board the ships, many of whom died of disease on the way.

tracts with wealthy settlers to work as servants or laborers for a long period of time. This practice was initiated in Virginia on July 30, 1619, when the House of Burgesses passed legislation legalizing "white servitude." And among the Pilgrim colonists arriving in Massachusetts Bay in 1620 were eighteen indentured servants.

It was as indentured servants that the first shipload of twenty Africans was brought to Jamestown, Virginia, near the end of August of 1619. Like other bondservants, after the period of their contract was concluded, they received their freedom and were granted land and full rights as citizens of Virginia.

This is not to suggest that the African slave trade did not exist at this time, only that it did not yet exist in the North American colonies. It was already flourishing in the Spanish and Portuguese colonies in the Caribbean and in Central and South America, and had been since 1517, when Bartolome de Los Casas asked the Spanish king for permission to import Africans to Hispaniola as slaves because the Indian slaves were all dying off from the hardship of their servitude. (The Africans were considered much hardier than the Native Americans.)

Although the king granted permission,

Spain was not allowed to participate in the African slave trade. In May of 1493, Pope Alexander VI (Roderigo Borgia, father of the infamous Lucrezia and Cesare) had issued a Papal Bull dividing the "heathen world" between Spain and Portugal. Most of the territory on the American continents was granted to Spain, while Portugal was given hegemony over all of Africa, including responsibility for the slave trade.

The English, Dutch, and French had to work out agreements with Portugal to gain rights to participate in the lucrative business of selling human beings.

The first of the English colonies to legalize slavery was Massachusetts, which passed its law in December of 1641, a full twenty years before a southern state, Virginia, enacted a law to permit the institution. For 142 years, slavery flourished in Massachusetts, not being outlawed until 1783, at the end of the American Revolution, and only eighty years before Abraham Lincoln issued the Emancipation Proclamation.

However, it took a number of years for slavery in its later known form to become institutionalized. The legislative bodies of the colonies constantly debated, defined, and formalized the concept. One of the major justifications for slavery at the time was that

African blacks were "heathens," and there were numerous cases of slaves converting to Christianity. After the Restoration of the Stuart monarchy in England in 1660, the British courts decreed that infidel slaves had to be freed if they converted to Christianity. This presented both a moral and an economic dilemma for the colonies.

Virginia presents one example. In 1667, to counteract the British court decision, the colony passed a law stating that individuals born in slavery did not end their servitude by conversion to Christianity, but in 1670 it altered that law to decree that slaves who had become Christians before being imported were not to be subjected to lifelong servitude but were to be treated as indentured servants. Then, twelve years later, the burgesses repealed the 1670 law. In 1705, the matter was brought up again, and it was decreed that all imported servants were to be bound for life. Excepted were those who had been Christians in their native land or who had lived free in a Christian country. This limited slavery to blacks and applied to almost all of them. Exempted were "Turks and Moors in amity with Her Majesty."

Although the largest number of slaves were in the southern colonies and in the Caribbean, where they worked the sugar, rice, and indigo plantations, slavery was not a rarity in New England, as some have suggested. It was so common that, in 1687, a Frenchman visiting Boston reported: "You may also own negroes and negresses; there is not a house in Boston however small may be its means that has not one or two. There are those that have five or six, and all make a good living."

Initially the New Englanders did not have much actual use for African slave labor except as household servants, for most did not possess skills they considered useful in their trades. The great value of the Africans to the leading financiers of Boston lay in the buying and selling of them. They were merely a commodity to complete the third part of the "triangle trade" of molasses, rum, and slaves from Boston to Barbados to the African west coast and back to Boston, saving their ships from the necessity of returning from Africa on the "middle passage" with their holds empty.

The morality of slavery did not matter to the merchants and traders of Boston at this time. In the ten years between 1755 and 1765, they sold 23,743 slaves through Massachusetts, though the slave population of the colony in 1765 was only 5,779, indicating that most went to other colonies, pri-

Long before the African slave trade reached the colonies of North America, it flourished in Africa and the Middle East. Whole communities were established in some parts of Africa

for conducting the extensive business of blacks selling blacks
from other tribes. The first Africans slaves in the New World
were taken to the colonies of South and Central America.

marily to the South. The profits went into the pockets of the proper Bostonians whose descendants, in the next century, would lead the crusade of abolition against the southern slave-owners.

Meanwhile, during the middle of the eighteenth century, as they discovered that not all Africans were "savages," that some possessed skills or crafts of commercial value and others could be taught, the New Englanders began to use slaves for other than household servants or farm laborers. Ropemaking was an especially useful craft because of the extensive use of rope in the rigging of the ships in the seafaring industry. Weaving skills were helpful in the cloth manufactories. Some slaves knew how to work with clay and were of use in the making of pottery and china.

At the same time, the slave owners and slave traders of New England began to realize that there were a number of problems with slavery, problems that ultimately made the institution uneconomical or unprofitable. The slaves were not especially happy with the system. Unlike indentured servants, most of whom accepted their positions of servitude because they were "voluntary," slaves were constantly looking for opportunities to escape from a servitude they had not agreed to. When they succeeded in getting away, their owners faced a loss of their investment.

But the most serious problems arose from the slave trade itself. There were risks, dangers, and hazards in bringing shiploads of live cargo from Africa that often proved economically disastrous for the ship owners. Increasingly the ship captains risked their lives and those of their crews by sailing to and from Guinea and the Gold Coast, where Spanish and Portuguese pirates and privateers lay in wait to attack. Sailing up the Gambia or the Sierra Leone rivers or landing at the slave trading posts upriver, they were also taking the chance of being attacked by native African tribes.

One surviving account of these problems is that of the *Jolly Batchelor*, a ship belonging to a consortium headed by Peter Faneuil, for whom Boston's Faneuil Hall is named, printed in the *Boston Evening Post* on August 15, 1743:

> We now have certain Advice, that Capt. John Cutler, late Commander of a Snow belonging to this Town, who sailed for Guinea some time ago as he was trading in the River Sierra Leona, was murdered, with 2 or 3 of his Men, by some

Portuguese who are settled on that River. They rifled the Vessel, and took away his Slaves, etc., but by the Assistance of an honest English Man who is settled in those Parts, some of the Slaves were recovered, and the Vessel again fitted for the Sea, and last Friday she was brought into Newport by Captain Wickham of that Place, who had himself been taken by a Spanish Privateer on the Coast of Guinea some time before.

The most serious problem, however, was that of disease—smallpox, measles, diphtheria, yellow fever, typhoid. Not only did a large percentage of the precious cargo of Africans chained up in the holds of the ships die of these diseases, but so did the members of the crew and—if the ships reached harbor with the disease—so did many of the residents of the port cities. Typical of many slavers was the report of the *Mermaid*, which arrived off the coast of Boston in July of 1739 and was not allowed to pull into port because of rampant disease:

John Robinson, Master of the Schooner Mermaid from the Coast of Guinea, being sent for appear'd...and being Examin'd, on oath, Declares...That he came from the River Gambo, two and forty days ago, with Eleven White Men on board and Fifty Slaves; That they had the Small Pox, on board, five Months ago, for about Ten Weeks, one Hundred and Forty Leagues up the River Gambo; that he buried Two Whites and one Black; that afterwards he burnt Brimstone in the Vessel and Cleansed her with all possible care Vizt. in February last, Since which no Person has been Sick of that Distemper, but that they have had the Measles and the Flux on board, that the Flux continues among the Slaves, but the Measles is not now among them, that they have lost fifteen Slaves of the Flux, in the said River and in their Passage and that they buried two in sight of Cape Cod, Yesterday; That 3 Whites and 4 Blacks have had the Small Pox, that all the White men on board have had the Small Pox; That the Negroes are all young under Twenty years of age; That he took out all his Water Casks and Cleansed them, but the Ballast had not been shifted.

A few of the slaves chose to commit suicide, either by jumping overboard during the brief periods they were allowed on deck for air and exercise or by "swallowing" their tongues while chained below. But these were in the minority; most of the suicides were natives of Calabar, so the slavers generally came to avoid purchasing them.

As long as only a small percentage of cargo and crew died on the voyage across the middle passage, the Massachusetts and Rhode Island slave traders continued to be able to maintain a decent profit margin, and that was what was most important in continuing the traffic. They could buy a slave in Africa for about $25 and resell in America for about $150 to $200, depending upon age, health, and skills. As it did not cost much to feed them on the four or five week passage, the traders were not yet losing money. They could afford to lose about a fourth of their cargo and still make a profit.

However, it is important to realize that only about four percent of the overall slave trade went to the North American colonies. The largest number, thirty-two percent, were taken to the Portuguese colonies of South America, and twenty-four percent went to the British West Indies. An additional seventeen percent were taken to the French West Indies and thirteen percent to the Spanish West Indies and Central America. Of the remainder, seven percent were traded to the Dutch colonies in South America, three

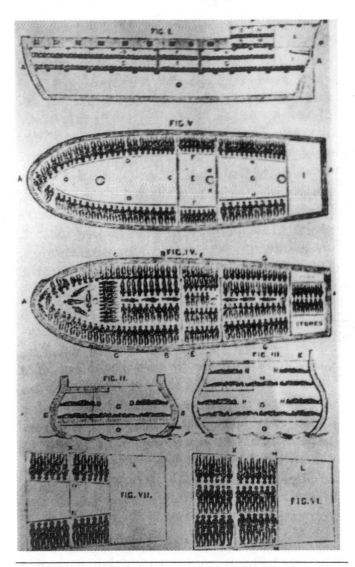

As can be seen in the above cross-section views of a slave ship, the slaves being transported across the Atlantic to the New World were packed in so tightly they barely had room to move.

percent to England, and two percent to the east coast of Africa and to Asia.

Yet when people think of black slavery, they think only of North America, and especially the South, perhaps because of the bloody civil war that brought an end to the institution.

Little has been written about the conditions of slavery in Massachusetts. It is probably true that Yankee slaves did not suffer as much hardship as did the southern slaves. Although New England winters were harsh, they were less deadly than southern summers. However, it is unlikely that the Yankee slave owners were any more considerate of their property than the plantation masters and overseers, especially since the Puritans had a death sentence for "heresy," which was believing in anything other than the Puritan religion, and meted out very strict punishment for not attending church services.

The slave system in Massachusetts was at its height when Prince Attucks was brought there from Africa, and he could not have been happy with his new status. From the fact that he was given the name "Prince," it can be assumed that he had been born the son of a tribal chieftain in Africa. He was of a very tall and powerful build, a fact that suggests he may have been a Fulani or a Tuareg.

At the time he entered into captivity, he was a young man probably in his teens. The slavers were undoubtedly English or New England colonists, for in 1713 Britain was granted the *asiento*, or right to manage the African slave trade, by the Treaty of Utrecht, which ended Queen Anne's War against the French, and which also opened up the French West Indies to colonial trade, making molasses cheaper and increasing New England's production of rum, the currency used for the purchase of African slaves.

After enduring the humiliation of the trip from Africa to Massachusetts, Prince Attucks was sold from shipboard to a white man from the vicinity of Framingham. There he spent the rest of his life as a farm laborer, and there he met the Indian woman Nancy who was to bear him a son named Crispus.

Chapter Three

Runaway

BY 1723, WHEN CRISPUS Attucks was
born, the institution of slavery in the North
American colonies had been formalized, and
new concepts of white supremacy as a
replacement for Christian supremacy were
growing. That year, in Virginia, the
Burgesses passed a law taking the right to
vote away from free blacks who owned property, the first known law based purely on
color. At about the same time, Massachusetts
enacted a law placing a bounty on Indian
scalps, paying one hundred pounds for each
scalp a colonist delivered. The first known

*There is no portrait of Crispus Attucks drawn or painted during
his lifetime. However, physical descriptions have survived, and
several artists have followed them to create portraits.*

scalping of Indians by white men occurred in 1725 by Captain Lovewell of Wakefield, New Hampshire, who delivered ten scalps to Boston to collect his bounty.

It must have been very difficult for young Crispus growing up half black and half Indian, both races reviled by the powerful whites of Massachusetts. And as a young child he was probably looked down upon by the Indians of Natick, among whom he lived.

"Natick" is not an Indian tribal name but a place name. The "Natick Indians" were in reality of two tribes, the Waban and the Nonatum, a part of the group who spoke the Algonquin language. They were the first of the New England tribes to be converted to Christianity by the white settlers, becoming known as "praying Indians," and because of it they had a very sad and tragic history.

In 1651, the proselytizing Puritan John Eliot established them in a "praying town" at Natick on the Charles River, as a part of a program of "civilizing" them. The code that Eliot drew up for them to follow obliged them to observe the sabbath, to be monogamous, to pay debts owed to the English, to give up murder, theft, and fornication, and to wear their hair "comely as the English do." A church and a school were established for them in 1660, and the following year his

MAMUSSE
WUNNEETUPANATAMWE
UP-BIBLUM GOD
NANEESWE
NUKKONE TESTAMENT
KAH WONK
WUSKU TESTAMENT.

Ne quoshkinnumuk nashpe Wuttinneumoh *CHRIST*
noh asoowesit

JOHN ELIOT·

CAMBRIDGE·
Printeuoopnashpe *Samuel Green* kah *Marmaduke Johnson.*
1 6 6 3.

John Eliot translated the Bible into the Algonquin language and
attempted to convert the New England tribes to Christianity. He
met with some success, and the "praying Indians," as they
became known, settled at the town of Natick, west of Boston.

The figure of the Indians fort or Palizado in
NEW ENGLAND
And the maner of the destroying
It by Captayne Vnderhill
And Captayne Mason

The Indians houses

Captayne Mason

Slavery in the North American colonies did not begin with the
importing of Africans but with the capture and export of Indians
to the Caribbean colonies after the Pequot War. Above is a

diagram depicting the attack by the colonists on the Pequot fort.
The Puritans did not consider the Indians to be "civilized" or
worthy of freedom and equality because they were not Christians.

translation of the Bible in Algonquin was published.

If the Natick Indians thought their conversion and their attempts to coexist with the white settlers would make their lives easier, they were mistaken.

In 1675, when war broke out between the Massachusetts settlers and the Indians, the conflict known as "King Philip's War," a group of the Natick Indians agreed to serve as scouts for the colonists, but a few also joined the Indians who followed Philip. Because the whites were fearful of all Indians, the remainder were imprisoned on Deer Island in Massachusetts Bay, where they survived through a harsh winter with little shelter or clothing, subsisting on clams and shellfish dug from the sandy beaches. Despite this cruel treatment from the whites, they continued in the Christian religion.

"King Philip" was a Pokanoket Indian, whose original name was Metacomet. He was the younger son of Massasoit, the chief of the Wampanoags, who had befriended the Plymouth colonists, maintaining a peace with them for forty years. However, his son Wamsutta married the daughter of the Pocasset sachem, unifying the tribes from Cape Cod to Narragansett Bay, which frightened the colonists. After the death of

Massasoit, the two sons went to the colonists at Plymouth to ask that they be given English names as a sign of their friendship. Wamsutta was given the name Alexander, and Metacomet was given the name Philip.

Despite this gesture, not long afterward the General Court at Plymouth began to grow nervous at the power of the Indians and sent two messengers to Alexander to bring him for questioning. The messengers, sons of Edward Winslow and William Bradford, burst in on Alexander and his family with guns raised, threatening to kill him if he did not accompany them to Plymouth.

Indignantly the chief refused; he was then roughed up and forced to go with the two young men. Alexander was so upset that, on the way to Plymouth, he developed a fever, which worsened as he was interrogated by the Court. Finally he was sent toward home on a litter but died before getting there.

Philip became chieftain of the unified tribes, and after what had happened to his brother he was distrustful of the colonists, who were intruding increasingly on land they had promised the friendly Indians. Bitterly he stated, "I am determined not to live till I have no country."

An uneasy peace existed between the Wampanoags and the colonists for almost ten years, despite the fact that the Plymouth Court continually called Philip to question him about suspected hostile activities. Eventually, in 1671, Philip and the colonists signed a peace treaty at Taunton, renewing their vow of friendship.

The chief counselor to Philip had been a Natick Indian named John Sassamon, who had also served Alexander in that capacity. Sassamon was a peaceable man; he had served as Eliot's assistant at Natick, being both a schoolteacher and a Christian missionary to his people. However, after a time, he renounced his Christianity and went back to live among the Wampanoags. Then, in 1674, he was persuaded by the whites to return to Natick, where he supposedly revealed to the colonists that Philip was planning war against them.

In January of 1675, Sassamon's body was found dead in a pond not far from the Plymouth settlement. Though they had no real proof, the colonists claimed that three agents of Philip had murdered Sassamon, one of whom was an important counselor to Philip. The three Wampanoags were arrested, tried, and hanged.

The Wampanoags began to arm themselves, joined by Narragansetts, Cowesits, and Pocassets. Late that summer they began to attack the colonial settlements of Rehoboth, Taunton, Swansea, and Dartmouth. Other New England tribes began to join with Philip, and more colonial towns were burned, with the war spreading to Connecticut and Rhode Island. Most of the Indian tribes who agreed to remain at peace with the colonists were captured and sold into slavery in the Indies. The "praying Indians" at Natick were taken under arms and confined at Deer Island for the duration of the war.

Gradually, after numerous bloody battles, the various tribes surrendered or were defeated, but Philip held out. Finally, in August 1676, he was killed and beheaded, with his head carried into Plymouth on a pike to be paraded before the townspeople.

With all of the other New England Indians killed, defeated, or sold into slavery, the praying Indians were permitted to leave Deer Island and return to Natick to take up their simple farming lives again. Two generations later a child of these people named Nancy grew to maturity and mated with a slave named Prince Attucks, bringing forth a child named Crispus.

Young Crispus attended church, where he was taught the Christian religion, and he attended the Natick school, where he was taught to read and write. It is clear that he accepted the religious principles and the new concepts of freedom and democracy espoused by John Locke that were filtering over from Great Britain. Yet as a child of two races that were denied the full benefits of the white man's religion and political system, he could not have helped but perceive the hypocrisy inherent in both.

It is not known at precisely what age Crispus was taken away from the Natick village and placed into slavery, or under what circumstances. He was definitely enslaved by age eleven, for it is reported that he was eleven when he decided he did not like slavery and would not endure it forever. He may have been enslaved at the time or he may have made his decision based upon what he had witnessed of his father's servitude. Crispus must have shown his dissatisfaction to his masters, for by the time he was twenty-seven he had been sold five times, lasting only a short time with each owner.

The problem for New England slaves wishing to escape during this period was that there were few places they could run and hope to survive. In later years, when slavery was strictly a southern institution, runaways could find a haven in the North. In the eighteenth century, when slavery was observed

A leader of the Pocassets and Wampanoags, Metacomet took the name Philip as a gesture of friendship toward the white settlers, but the colonists continued to fear his power over the tribes of Massachusetts and finally provoked him to war against them.

throughout the colonies, runaways had only two choices: they could take their chances in the wilderness to the west, the Indian territories, or they could try to find a sympathetic shipmaster who would sign them on and take them to sea.

Neither alternative offered much hope for successful escape. Chances of survival in the western territory were slim. Although most of the Indian tribes pitied the black slaves, most would not offer assistance, distrusting all of the foreigners who had invaded their land. Without aid, runaways had difficulty finding food and shelter, critical in the harsh northern winters.

Most escaping slaves attempted to go to sea; however, the likelihood of recapture was high. Although shipmasters were always in need of strong, able-bodied crewmen and they generally did not have many scruples about where the men came from, slave owners usually offered generous rewards for the return of their property, and the law punished anyone aiding or abetting escaping slaves. Furthermore, the first places that slave owners or slave-catchers looked for the runaways were the docks of the major ports—Boston, Salem, Providence, or New London.

Indeed, it is because of this that a partial record of Crispus Attucks' escape has survived. His owner at the time, William Brown of Framingham, placed an advertisement in the Boston *Gazette* on October 2, 1750, which read:

> Ran away from his Master William Brown of Framingham, on the 30th of Sept. last, a Molatto Fellow, about 27 Years of Age, named Crispas, 6 Feet two Inches high, short curl'd Hair, his Knees nearer together than common; had on a light colour'd Bearskin Coat, plain brown Fustian jacket, or brown all-Wool one, new Buckskin Breeches, blue Yarn Stockings, and a check'd woollen Shirt.
>
> Whoever shall take up said Runaway, and convey him to his abovesaid master, shall have ten Pounds, old Tenor Reward, and all necessary Charges paid. And all Masters of Vessels and others, are hereby caution'd against concealing or carrying off said Servant on Penalty of the Law. Boston, October 2, 1750.

Some historians have referred to Attucks' owner as "Deacon" William Brown. However, according to the Framingham town records, Brown was not a deacon but plain "mister." The title of "deacon" may have been given to him to convey the appearance of Christian rectitude. But the records that have survived suggest that Brown was anything but a sympathetic man.

When William Brown purchased his farm near the town of Framingham in the late 1740s, it included a rural schoolhouse, one of two schools supported by Framingham, the other being in town. Brown objected to the presence of the school on his property and petitioned to have it removed. Interestingly, the controversy over the school came to a head in the year just prior to Crispus Attucks' escape, and it may be more than mere coincidence in light of the fact that Attucks had been educated.

At the Framingham town meeting of March 4, 1750, it was "Voted that Lieut. Wane Mixer, Messers William Brown, John Trowbridge, Mark Whitney & Joseph Buckminster be a Committee to order the affair of [the] school's moving."

Sometime during the summer, the school was removed from Brown's farm, and at the end of September, Attucks ran away.

It was logical for Brown to assume that Crispus would go to Boston. Only twenty miles away from Framingham, it was the major metropolis of the colonies, having a population at this time of over fifteen thousand and being the most important port. If a slave could get there and succeed in signing aboard or stowing away, he might be able to make it to a new colony just established in the South the year before, where slavery and rum were outlawed. This was the colony of Georgia, where England was sending its criminals and prostitutes to colonize. (However, when its anti-slavery position became an impediment to progress, it was revoked.)

Crispus was shrewd enough not to do the expected thing. Aided by friends and family at Natick, he obtained a change of clothing and made his way to Nantucket, an island more than ninety miles to the southeast, inhabited by Quakers who were doing a thriving business in the whaling industry.

Chapter Four

A Seafaring Man

AS WHALING IS A violent, even war-like industry, it would seem to be an odd, even an incompatible, occupation for peace-able Quakers. However, in the early eigh-teenth century the colonial whaling industry, centering around Nantucket Island and Buzzard's Bay, was almost entirely run by members of the religious sect. These settle-ments developed a special race of "fighting Quakers," or what Herman Melville called "Quakers with a vengeance."

The official name for Quakers is "Friends." They came to be called "Quakers" because

At left is a typical seaman of the period when Crispus Attucks ran away from home and went to sea. Although this rather ideal-ized depiction shows a white man, many were black or Indian.

the founder of their faith, George Fox, told them to "tremble at the word of the Lord." Other Christian sects considered them peculiar and looked down upon them because they were stubbornly mild-mannered and irascibly peaceable. They were also strongly opposed to slavery, the first of the American colonists to speak out against the institution.

The Quakers were greatly hated by the Puritans of Massachusetts Bay, as well as by their compatriots back in England. In fact, the Boston Puritans did everything possible to try to prevent the heretical sect from finding a haven in the new world, especially in New England, even though the earliest Quakers were sent there by the English Puritans, who in 1649 had gained control of the British government, executed King Charles I, and outlawed the British monarchy, establishing a "Protectorate" under Lord Cromwell, which lasted until 1660.

The first Quakers arrived in Boston in July 1656, two women named Mary Fisher and Anne Austin who arrived aboard the *Swallow*. They were jailed by the Bostonians, who quickly enacted a statute outlawing Quakerism and imposing a fine on any ship owner or ship captain who transported members of the sect to the colony. The two women were then released and shipped to Barbados, with the understanding that they could not return to Boston. However, no sooner had Boston gotten rid of them than eight more Quakers arrived. These were swiftly returned to England.

In 1658, the city banished a Quaker couple, Lawrence and Cassandra Southwick, but would not permit their two young children—a boy named Daniel and a girl named Provided—to accompany them because they hoped to "save their souls." When the children refused to attend Puritan church services, the Boston authorities attempted to sell them as slaves (for ten pounds each) in the Indies, but no ship's captain would transport them.

So virulent was the hatred of the Puritans for the Quakers that in 1660, Mary Dyer was sentenced to death in Boston for being an "unrepentant" Quaker. For that reason most of the early Quakers in New England sought refuge in Rhode Island, the colony created by Roger Williams and his Baptist followers, who had enacted a law for religious tolerance after their banishment by the Puritans.

Although Nantucket and Buzzard's Bay were a part of Massachusetts, they were closer to Rhode Island than they were to Boston, being south and west of Cape Cod, and the boundaries of the colonies were not well defined at the time, so the Quakers felt safe in settling there.

It is not precisely clear how they came to dominate the whaling industry. The earliest whalers of New England were Puritans, who depended entirely upon finding carcasses that had been stranded on the beaches, though a few venturesome sailors hunted close to shore. The true beginning of whale-hunting in the area dates from 1712, when Christopher Hussey, of Providence, Rhode Island, was blown out to sea by a strong northerly wind, thought to be lost by his friends and family. While at sea, Hussey saw and killed a sperm whale, which he lashed to his boat and managed to convey back to shore. This convinced the local whalers that they could venture into the deep water to hunt, and the industry burgeoned.

The first whaling fishery had already been established at Nantucket by the Quakers in 1690. By 1715, it consisted of six whaling sloops, and by 1750, when Crispus Attucks arrived there, it had grown to well over a hundred. It had also established several "trying houses," establishments where whale oil was extracted from the blubber by cooking it in huge kettles. The stench from this process was so severe, capable of being smelled from many miles around, that none of the more

The Puritans of New England hated the Quakers and tried to keep them out of their colonies, jailing them, executing them, and selling them into slavery. The Quakers of Nantucket offered the first safe haven for runaway New England slaves.

established and more refined communities would permit the industry. It may have been this factor that made Nantucket Island the ideal place for the center of activity and enabled the Quakers to pursue it without interference from the proper Bostonians.

However, whaling was very lucrative for the New England economy. The useful commodities sold locally and transported to England were sperm oil and whale oil, shipped in barrels and used for lighting, heating, and cooking, and whale bone, accounted in pounds, which provided fibers for brushes, sieves, umbrellas, and corsets.

From the very beginning, whalers recruited blacks as seamen, along with Indians, partly because the Quakers were opposed to slavery and racial prejudice and partly because the whaling seafarers were considered the lowest rung of the social ladder, even lower than merchant seamen, who referred to whalers as "blubber boilers."

The work was filthy and hazardous, and crews were treated brutally, so experienced white sailors without a criminal record or some other socially unacceptable character fault generally sought employment on other kinds of sailing vessels. Whaling ships of the time have been described as "a place of refuge for the distressed and persecuted, a school for the dissipated, an asylum for the needy."

It seemed an ideal way for a runaway slave like Crispus Attucks to succeed at his escape. Even if "Deacon" Brown came looking for him in Nantucket, the Quakers were not likely to turn Crispus in, even if he revealed his identity to them, for their religion required them to assist in defeating slavery. So opposed to the institution were the Quakers that in 1696, their annual meeting warned the sect's members that they could be expelled for aiding in the slave trade in any way. The admonition was issued that particular year because the monopoly of the Royal African Trade Company was terminated and the trade was opened up to ships from New England.

It seems likely, however, that Crispus was going under an assumed name. Whether he was using the alias "Michael Johnson" at this point is not known, though this was the name he claimed in 1770 at the time of the Boston Massacre. In the twenty years between his escape and his death, he probably used several different names. From the very beginning, however, it seems clear that he attempted to pass as a full-blooded Indian in order to escape detection as a runaway.

The choice of "Johnson" as a last name was probably deliberate. Several related Johnson

Crispus Attucks went to work aboard a Quaker whaling ship and gradually worked his way up through the ranks to the level of harpoonist. Whaling was arduous and unpleasant work, however,

and it could be quite dangerous. When struck by the first harpoon, the whale would dive into the depths of the ocean, then rise to the surface again, often overturning the small rowboats.

families were quite prominent in Framingham during the years when Crispus Attucks was growing up, and they all had children roughly the same age as Crispus. One, the Caleb Johnson family, had a daughter named Dorothy who was exactly the age of Crispus; and Nathaniel Johnson's son Nathaniel was only four years older.

It is entirely possible that one of the Johnsons aided Attucks in his escape and he chose the name out of respect and gratitude.

Physically, Crispus was just what the whalers wanted as a seaman, though he was probably considerably older than most of his fellow sailors. They sought out "tall, stalwart men," who were both agile and strong; at six feet two inches tall, Crispus certainly fit the bill. And they did not even attempt to recruit experienced sailors but sought out boys from the farms of New England, as well as from Cape Cod and Long Island, who dreamed of romance and excitement in a life at sea.

These recruits were promised a percentage of the catch, a small fraction of the total for those on the lowest level, and they were given an advance against the catch to start, an outfit of clothes, and their board and lodging aboard ship. Since their expenses were deducted from the advances, beginning whalers rarely saw any actual cash from

Crispus Attucks became proficient in the use of the harpoon, as did many other blacks in the eighteenth and nineteenth centuries. In 1848, a toggle harpoon was invented by Lewis Temple, an African American of New Bedford, Massachusetts.

their promised funds.

Crispus began his seafaring career as an ordinary seaman, working the decks and rigging on the whale-hunting voyages, then rowing one of the small boats used in the harpooning and capture of the massive creatures. However, he quickly worked his way up through boat-steerer to being a headsman or harpooner, the most dangerous of jobs and one of the most skilled and appreciated.

At the time Crispus began his sailing career, most whaling ships were sloops, single-masted boats that were rigged fore and aft, with a single headsail, but some sloops were being rigged as snows, having two masts. They were generally about twenty-seven feet in length, built sharp at both ends, and they carried between four and six whale-boats. A good crew numbered about twenty-eight, including, besides the captain, three mates, two boatswains, a carpenter, a blacksmith, a cooper, and a cook.

The whaling ships were at sea for about six weeks a cruise. For the ordinary seaman, life aboard ship was difficult. The officers were brutal, and conditions in the forecastle were cramped. The men took turns at watch, generally in pairs, and the turns up in the "crow's nest" were long and boring, requiring the man on duty to keep an eye out for whales on the horizon day and night.

When a whale was sighted, the rest of the crew had to be alerted. Then the whaleboats were lowered, each with six men, four to row, one to steer and one to serve as headsman or harpooner to carry out the attack on the whale. When a whale was first hit by a harpoon, it would descend, so there had to be sufficient line on the harpoon to take care of the depth. The greatest danger to the seamen was during this time between the descent and the whale's subsequent rise to the surface, when it would be harpooned again.

Once killed, the whale would be lashed to the ship itself and the blubber removed by peeling off in strips or in a single spiral strip if the ship was equipped with an apparatus for turning the whale. The blubber was stored in the ship's hold, along with the spermaceti and the whalebone, to be transported back to shore for processing.

Crispus worked aboard the whaling ships for a period of five or six years, leaving at some point during the French and Indian War, known in Europe as the Seven Years War. His reason for making a change is not known. He may have seen the war as an opportunity to rise above the station of a whaler, to sign on as a sailor in the navy or a merchant ship, or it could have been due to the fact that the Quakers reduced their whale-hunting during periods of war, avoiding situations in which they might be drawn into conflicts.

The French and Indian War was essentially the first phase of a longer conflict between England and France for control of worldwide colonial empire, that first phase being for control of the North American continent, with the second phase taking place in India, the Philippines, and the Caribbean. The American phase of the war, which took place between 1754 and 1760, was called "French and Indian" because France had as its ally the vast Iriquois Confederacy in trying to drive the English colonists out of the new world. The Iriquois occupied territory in upstate New York and around the Great Lakes. The Algonquin speaking tribes from whom Crispus was descended through his mother sided with the English.

The conflict began in May 1754, when Lieutenant Colonel George Washington, in charge of colonial militia at Great Meadow in Pennsylvania, was forced by the French to retreat and set up a new encampment at Fort Necessity. The war was responsible for making the career of George Washington. The

American phase ended with the British defeating the French on the Plains of Abraham and then taking Montreal in 1760.

Although most major battles took place on land, the war was also waged at sea, and the British made use of whaleboats for landing ground troops, a precursor of modern-day marines. It is believed that Crispus Attucks made the transition from whaler to merchant seaman by a short stint in the British or colonial navy, operating one of the whaleboats.

Somehow Crispus did make that difficult transition, for during the 1760s he not only worked as a sailor on merchant vessels under the name of Michael Johnson, but rose to the rank of boatswain. Although he was thought to be an Indian by his employers, he had the advantage of being able to read and write and he was quite intelligent.

He also had an aura of authority and a natural capability for leadership and was liked and trusted by the sailors he supervised. When he spoke, other men listened, and he often voiced his strong political views about freedom and justice.

These were the qualities of his personality that would, in time, bring him briefly to fame—or notoriety—in history.

Chapter Five

A Rebellious
Spirit

AFTER THE END of the French and
Indian War, Crispus moved to Nassau in the
Bahamas, establishing himself at New
Providence as a home base. By this time he
was definitely using the name Michael
Johnson. It is not known if he ever married
and had a family, but if he did so it would
have been at this time and under this alias.
He signed aboard merchant ships trading
between the Caribbean islands, the eastern
seaboard of the North American colonies, and
England.

Like most sailing men, he was able to see

*During the French and Indian War, the British army made good
use of whaleboats, as depicted in this painting of British troops
landing at the cliffs below the Plains of Abraham.*

the world from a rather broad perspective. When ships were in port, sailors spent much of their time in taverns and public houses, where much of the talk was of politics, especially during this period when governments were changing radically.

The concepts of democracy, of representative government, were still relatively new, having grown out of the English Revolution. With the removal of the Stuart kings, the British monarchy had been stripped of much of its power; an elected Parliament and royal ministers now governed England and its colonies. Although the colonies had their own local representative legislative bodies, these were largely "advisory," with little real power, subject to the dictates of Parliament in London and to the autocratic decisions of its appointed governors.

At its inception, the concept of democracy was not quite as we define it in the twentieth century. The right to vote and participate in government was granted only to a few, those who were "enlightened"—property owners and those of high or noble birth, who were "Christians" of whatever sect was currently in power. Historically, the era was known as the "Enlightenment," and it was a time when knowledge—or at least the ability to read and write—was becoming more widespread, no longer just a privilege of kings and church leaders. With an increase in knowledge came an increased desire of the "enlightened" to govern themselves.

Many people still believed in the "divine right of kings" to rule, especially the kings themselves; however, an increasing number of people were believing in the "divine right of the enlightened" to govern, especially those who considered themselves enlightened. The number of different Christian sects was growing, with each thinking it knew more than others and therefore had a greater right to govern. The only thing they all agreed on was that they knew more than the uneducated and the "heathens," such as the Africans and the Native Americans.

It was therefore easy for the English citizens and their parliament to exclude colonists from participation in government. Not only were a great many of them exiles of one sort or another, but initially they had been permitted to go to the colonies to serve commercial interests, as "employees" or representatives of trading companies. The insular British failed to perceive that, with the passage of more than a hundred years, cities had grown up in the colonies and many colonists were no longer serving the organized "companies."

The English attitude was similar to that of masters toward servants or of slave-owners toward slaves. The colonists were *serving* the voting classes of the mother country, and they were treated accordingly.

The lower classes in the colonies—the slaves and indentured servants—understood this attitude very well. When people like Samuel Adams, Patrick Henry, and John Hancock began to talk of freedom and human rights, they were among the first to respond to the revolutionary call. Historians who suggest that Crispus Attucks did not understand what he was doing when he faced off with British troops are naive. He understood very well what he was fighting for. Although he had only a few years of formal education, he had gained much knowledge of world affairs through many evenings in the public houses, taverns, and coffee houses in port cities such as Boston, Charleston, Kingston, and Liverpool, where politics and world events were a major topic of discussion.

The actions of the British that provoked the rebellious spirit among the colonists began not long after the conclusion of the Seven Years War, with the signing of the Treaty of Paris in 1763, though the injustices had their roots in English conflicts that had been going on for over a hundred years. Since shortly after the beginning of British colonization in North America, England had been in turmoil, first with the series of internal religious wars that are now referred to as the English Revolution, then with a series of conflicts with other European powers.

In 1649, after lengthy wars between Catholics and Protestants, the Puritans led by Cromwell beheaded King Charles I and declared the British monarchy at an end. Cromwell established himself as "Lord Protector" of the nation, and full powers for the enactment of laws were placed in the hands of Parliament. However, even he had problems with parliamentary rule, and for a time disbanded Parliament. After the death of Cromwell in 1660, it was felt that a single national leader was needed to guide policy, and Cromwell's son was deemed unworthy. Parliament restored the monarchy, allowing Charles II, the eldest son of the executed king, to assume the throne but with two important limitations: his power would be subject to the consent of Parliament; and, since the king was titular head of the Church of England, the succession of Protestant rulers would have to be maintained.

The Restoration, with its tenuous balance between monarchy and parliamentary democracy, worked during the reign of

Charles II, from 1660 to 1685. It was a period of prosperity and relative peace, though there were three wars with the Dutch during this time, one of which ended in 1667 with Britain gaining possession of the Dutch colony of New Amsterdam, renaming it New York.

However, when Charles died, his younger brother assumed the throne as James II, even though he was Catholic and believed in the divine right of kings to rule with full powers. In order to maintain its "democratic" power, Parliament called on the king's daughter Mary and her husband William of Orange, both Protestants, to overthrow James, which they succeeded in doing in 1689. Having ruled for only four years, James II did not abdicate but went into exile in France, where he sought the help of Catholic King Louis XIV in regaining his throne from his daughter and son-in-law.

During the next seventy-four years, England and France would go to war four separate times, under five separate British monarchs, and England would be invaded twice by Stuart pretenders to the throne, James' legitimate heirs, his son James III and his grandson "Bonnie" Prince Charlie, both of whom had a more valid claim to the throne by the old laws of primogeniture than

Oliver Cromwell established Puritan control in England in 1649, with himself serving as "Lord Protector" and Parliament as the ultimate lawmaking body for the country and its colonies. When the monarchy was reestablished, Parliament remained in control.

did the queens and kings who have held the throne ever since, but they were denied the throne because they were Catholic.

However, it was a new order, in which the English people governed themselves. During the reign of William and Mary, Britain was at war with France for eight years, reaching a peace with the Treaty of Ryswick in 1697. During the reign of Mary's younger sister Anne, they were at war with France for eleven years, winning victory with the Treaty of Utrecht in 1713.

When Queen Anne died in 1714, the Stuart line of the monarchy ended because the direct line was Catholic. Parliament had to go far afield to find an heir to the throne who was Protestant, importing the German Hanovers, installing the English-hating King George I on the throne. It was with King George I that the British government took its present form, not only having a democratically elected parliament but also having a prime minister as a chief policy maker. The prime minister during the reign of George I and during much of that of his son George II was Robert Walpole.

It was during the reign of George II and Prime Minister Walpole, when the new concept of "democracy" had been firmly established, that the serious troubles began between England and her North American colonies, though they did not break out into violence until William Pitt was prime minister. England seemed always to be at war during this period. In 1739, it was the War of Jenkins' Ear with Spain, so named because a Spanish sea captain had cut off the ear of an English sailor named Robert Jenkins, but actually it was over rights in the colonial slave trade. The following year began the War of the Austrian Succession against France, the Netherlands, and Germany, which concluded eight years later with the Treaty of Aix-la-Chapelle. After only eight years of peace, England went to war with France again, beginning the first phase of the Seven Years War, the French and Indian War in the North American colonies and Canada, the second phase finally concluding with the Treaty of Paris in 1763.

Even though most of these wars had been fought for economic gain or for dominance in colonial commerce, they had been costly and, as peace was finally being established, ways had to be found to pay for them. Taxation seemed the only solution; to avoid overburdening the citizens at home, upon whom the elected members of Parliament depended to hold office, a large percentage of the taxes were imposed on the colonists, who had no

The English Parliament passed all important laws governing the American colonies. The colonists objected to this in principle, but what ultimately caused resistance was the imposition of taxes on

everything imported to the colonies from England, from paper to tea. Here, William Pitt, one of the few friends the colonists had in the English government, addresses the House of Commons.

vote. After 1763 the rationalization was: the French and Indian War had been of considerable benefit to the North American colonies; therefore they ought to pay for it.

King George II had died in 1760, before the Seven Years War was over, and was succeeded by his grandson as George III, who had as his prime minster William Pitt. Although most historians portray the American Revolution as a quarrel between the colonists and King George III, it was actually a war between the colonists and the English Parliament. As much as George III attempted to regain some of the power relinquished by the earlier Stuarts and Hanovers, he was little more than a figurehead.

Parliament had levied its first direct tax on the colonies in 1733 with the Molasses Act. The major industry in New England at the time was the manufacture and export of rum, with well over a hundred major distilleries in the area. To make rum required molasses, which was imported from the West Indies. However, the British West Indies could provide only about one-fourth of what was needed, so the remainder had to come from the Dutch and French West Indies. The Molasses Act placed a duty of six pence a gallon on molasses imported from non-British colonies. Since the molasses cost only six

King George III is traditionally blamed for the abuses on the American colonies, yet he was largely a figurehead, and the real problems were created by his ministers and by Parliament.

pence a gallon in the first place, and it cost four pence a gallon to ship to New England, this was an outrageously high tax, and a great many sea captains plying the route between the Indies and Boston took to smuggling the precious commodity. In some cases, they did so with the complicity of the colonial customs officials, who accepted bribes to keep their mouths shut.

British officials largely ignored the practice until William Pitt sought to end it by the issuance of writs of assistance. These writs permitted government officials to inspect and even to appropriate the property of anyone suspected of concealing illicit goods. The officials could enter a home, business, warehouse, or ship and take possession merely on suspicion that the owner was concealing molasses, and the property owners had no right to prevent it, an invasion of privacy.

The colonists continued their smuggling activities but became more careful about hiding their contraband.

In 1764, in order to try to collect the taxes, Parliament passed a new measure, the Sugar Act, reducing the duty on molasses to three pence a gallon. It was thought that the colonists would accept this new act, which was recommended by George Grenville, the First Lord of the Treasury, because the tax

George Grenville, the First Lord of the Treasury, was responsible for many of the onerous taxes imposed upon the colonies, including the Sugar Act, the Stamp Act, and the Quartering Act.

was only slightly more than what they paid
as bribes and they would not be breaking the
law.

However, the act set forth other restric-
tions the colonists considered onerous, the
most objectionable being the paperwork that
shipmasters and sailors like Crispus Attucks
had to fill out, detailing every item in their
possession each time they entered a colonial
port. For ships that made stops in several
ports along the Atlantic seaboard, this was
ludicrous, and again it was an invasion of privacy.

This was only the beginning of the laws
and taxes that Grenville and Parliament
were to inflict on the colonists. Immediately
after the Sugar Act, Parliament passed the
Currency Act prohibiting the colonies from
using their own paper currency as legal ten-
der. In March 1765, Parliament passed the
Stamp Act, which placed a tax on all paper
and paper goods used by the colonists.
Everything from legal documents to newspa-
pers, diplomas, and playing cards had to bear
a stamp indicating that it had been purchased through an official of the Crown and
the tax had been paid. Two months later
came another act of Parliament, the
Quartering Act, requiring the colonies to provide quarters at their own expense for any

British troops sent there.

To make matters worse, the new laws took away the colonists' right to trial by jury or by a local judge who might be sympathetic; for any infractions of Grenville's tax measures, colonists would be tried by the British admiralty courts. This was a blatant statement by Parliament that British colonists were not equal to British citizens.

The rebellion in the colonies began immediately, with protests and newspaper articles appearing in cities north and south. Merchants in the major cities began a boycott of British goods, and ordinary citizens organized themselves into a group they called the "Sons of Liberty" to defy the new laws.

Most historians claim that the American Revolution was essentially a middle-class rebellion, pointing to the men who signed the Declaration of Independence as their proof, perhaps trying to dignify it. However, at its inception, all classes were involved in the Sons of Liberty, with a large number of the poor and working classes in the port cities participating. The mobs that went out in the summer and fall of 1765 to burn the stamp distributors in effigy and to attack their homes and offices were not composed only of lawyers, merchants, and artisans (though they did participate). A large percentage were servants, dockworkers, sailors, and apprentices—common people. Though there is no record of his involvement, as no "roll" of the members of the Sons of Liberty exists, it is likely that Crispus Attucks participated in the protests when he was in port.

The most dramatic protest by the Sons of Liberty occurred in Boston in August 1765, with what is called the "Stamp Act riot." A large mob of several thousand Bostonians hung an effigy of Andrew Oliver from the Liberty Tree, which stood at what is now the corner of Essex and Washington streets. Oliver was the stamp officer for Boston. The effigy and the mob remained there all day, while at the Town House the British governor and his council debated over what to do about the situation.

That evening, the mob cut down the effigy and paraded it to the Town House and into the chambers where the council was still discussing what to do. They then carried it out again, trooping down to the docks where Oliver had erected his stamp office. After destroying the building, the mob proceeded to a hill near Oliver's elegant mansion, where they burned the effigy.

While there, some of the mob began to attack the Oliver home, breaking windows and destroying his garden. Then others joined in, breaking into the house and destroying his furniture and possessions.

As a result of the riot, Oliver resigned. By the first of November, when the Stamp Act was to take effect, all of the stamp officers throughout the colonies had resigned. Not long afterward, Grenville resigned and the King appointed a new minister, the Marquis of Rockingham. In March 1766 Parliament repealed the Stamp Act. However, at the same time, it passed a Declaratory Act, proclaiming its right to make and enforce laws governing the colonies.

Word of the repeal of the Stamp Act reached Boston on May 16, and the citizens held a jubilant celebration in the streets on May 19. From this point on the words "freedom" and "liberty" were on everyone's lips, and they did not mean freedom and liberty only for the privileged or the middle class.

Evidence for this can be found in the fact that, on May 26, the Boston Town Meeting voting in favor of "the total abolishing of slavery from among us; that you [the council] move for a law, to prohibit the importation and purchasing of slaves for the future." Unfortunately the citizens had no power, and the governor and his council paid no heed to the people's "recommendation."

Chapter Six

Toward Freedom

THE FOUR YEARS following repeal of the Stamp Act would prove that the colonists had won only a reprieve, not a victory. Parliament and the ministers of George III were determined to show that they were the masters and the colonists their servants.

However, for a time, it appeared that the colonists had a defender if not a representative in England. In the summer of 1766, the King appointed William Pitt as his Prime Minister to replace Rockingham. Pitt had been the strongest voice in Parliament in

William Pitt was so sympathetic to the complaints of the colonists that he was frequently depicted with a kneeling black slave symbolizing the American colonies, as in this porcelain figurine.

opposition to the Stamp Act, claiming that colonists should have all the rights of British citizens and proclaiming that they were "the sons not the bastards of England" and that they were not "slaves." Indeed, it was in his speeches that the plight of the colonists was first compared to slavery, and in some of the political art of the time the American colonies were depicted as a prostrate black slave.

But by this time Pitt was old and in ill health. When he was forced to take to his bed, the power fell to the Chancellor of the Exchequer, Charles Townshend, who was no friend to the colonists.

Townshend picked up where Grenville had left off, determined not only to raise funds by taxing the colonies but also to show them their proper place. He proposed imposing duties on numerous products imported into the colonies from England—not just paper but also glass, lead, paint, oil, printer's ink, and tea. On June 29, 1767, Parliament passed the Townshend Acts. To attempt to end the problems of colonial smuggling, Townshend created a Board of Customs Commissioners and a new set of customs collectors for the colonial port cities. He also created a new government post, a Secretary of State for the Colonies, to which he had Wills Hill, the Earl of Hillsborough, appointed.

In February 1768, the Massachusetts House of Representatives, under the leadership of Samuel Adams, sent a letter to the legislatures of the other colonies calling for a united stand against the Townshend Acts by boycotting the taxable British goods. Most of the other colonies joined in the boycott.

To attempt to prevent the kind of riots and demonstrations that had defeated the Stamp Act, Townshend and Hillsborough sent four thousand British troops to Boston to protect the customs collectors. Called from their station at Halifax in Canada, the first of these troops arrived in Boston Harbor aboard British warships at the end of September 1768—nine companies of the Fourteenth and Twenty-ninth Regiments but with one of the Fifty-ninth.

By the Quartering Act of 1765, the colonists were required to provide quarters for the troops, as well as to pay for them. The Massachusetts Council insisted this gave them the right to determine where the troops would be quartered, and it insisted they be placed at Castle William, an island in the harbor, three miles away but technically part of the city of Boston. Lieutenant Colonel Dalrymple of the Fourteenth argued that a state of rebellion existed in Boston and therefore they would have to be quartered onshore,

After the citizens of Boston began to protest against the Stamp
Act by burning the stamp tax collectors in effigy and attacking
their homes, England sent four thousand troops to "maintain

order." Some of the troops were temporarily housed in tents set up on Boston Common, the park in the center of town. Naturally the citizens were outraged by the occupation of their city.

in the city proper. He also ordered that the warships be positioned with their guns directed at the city.

It was decided that the Fourteenth would be quartered in the Manufactory House and the Twenty-ninth could be temporarily set up in tents on Boston Common. On October 1, the troops stepped ashore and marched up King Street like a conquering army. But the tenants of the Manufactory House refused to vacate, so Dalrymple's men temporarily occupied Faneuil Hall and the Town House.

In November more British troops arrived from Ireland, having been delayed by heavy storms at sea. (Because of these storms some of the troops would not reach Boston until late in the spring of 1769.)

An uneasy peace was established in the city. The presence of the troops served their primary purpose, enabling the Royal Governor Francis Bernard to collect the customs duties. However, the duties remained small because the boycott of British goods continued. Neither the colonists nor the majority of the troops felt comfortable with the occupation of the city. Some of the troops deserted, aided by citizens; and some of the colonists, sympathizing with the hardships being endured by the common soldiers, made friends with them and offered them food and comfort. It was only a small percentage of soldiers who behaved in an arrogant and overbearing manner toward the Bostonians, but in a situation of this sort only a few difficulties proved too many.

There were frequent fist fights between citizens and off-duty soldiers, as well as numerous complaints from merchants that the soldiers would not pay their bills.

It was not just the troops on the street that caused problems for Boston. There was also the British war fleet in the harbor. By the spring of 1769, there had been so many desertions from the navy that not enough sailors remained to man the ships. Commander Samuel Hood, responsible for the fleet, issued an order for the ships' captains to blockade the harbor and to stop all British and colonial merchant vessels and to impress crew members into naval service. Even though there was a 1707 British law prohibiting this practice, this had been done to colonial merchant vessels during the French and Indian War.

It was a practice that was hated by the colonial seamen, as well as by their captains and ship's owners. Nevertheless the British fleet carried out the practice without facing any resistance until a brig, the *Pitt Packet* owned by Robert Hooper of Marblehead,

To insure that all import duties were paid by the colonists, British ships blockaded Boston Harbor, while troops maintained order on shore. However, morale was low among the sailors,

and so many deserted that the ships' captains began to stop merchant ships and impress members of their crews into naval service, a practice that was strictly against the law.

Massachusetts, attempted to elude a warship, the *Rose*, which gave chase and fired on the merchant vessel. Officers and men from the *Rose* boarded the *Pitt Packet* and attempted to impress members of its crew who had armed themselves and hidden in a small compartment below deck. When the armed naval men tried to take the crew by force, one crewman fired a musket, killing a young naval officer.

The *Pitt Packet* was impounded and its crew arrested. When brought to trial, the seaman who had fired the gun was defended by John Adams and James Otis on the basis of the 1707 law and was acquitted. It was a minor victory for the rights of the colonists, and it offered hope that conditions might improve.

In June there was another sign of hope. Some of the British troops, the Sixty-fourth and Sixty-fifth Regiments, were ordered to leave Boston for Halifax. Ironically—or perhaps intentionally—one of the ships chosen to transport the departing troops was the *Rose*. The Admiralty may have felt it would be tactful to get the unpleasant reminder away from Boston.

Yet two regiments remained in the city— the Fourteenth and the Twenty-ninth.

During the occupation, Crispus Attucks

sailed in and out of Boston several times, and he saw what was happening clearly during his days and evenings ashore. Like any merchant seaman he would have been apprehensive about the possibility of being impressed into the British navy. He had good friends in Boston, though most knew him as Michael Johnson and few realized that he was only a few miles from his original home.

When he was in Boston and on leave, he would get day work making ropes and cables for ships' riggings at John Gray's ropewalks.

The winter of 1769-1770 was a particularly harsh one in Boston, with frequent storms of snow and ice, causing a halt to ships sailing in and out of port. It is not known precisely when Crispus Attucks arrived in Boston on this trip, but he was certainly there by sometime in January of 1770, and his ship was unable to set sail again for South Carolina, its destination, throughout the month of February. He took day work at the ropewalks when it was available and when the weather permitted, and he spent his evenings at one of the taverns with his friends, generally the Royal Exchange, where he had taken a room.

During the fall and the frigid winter, tempers had been heating up in Boston, with increasing fights and brawls breaking out between colonists and soldiers. In September, attorney James Otis and customs commissioner John Robinson fought each other with walking sticks, resulting in serious head wounds to Otis. The Sons of Liberty had begun to paint graffiti on the stores and homes of merchants refusing to participate in the boycott of British goods. And the Daughters of Liberty, the women of Boston who had given up British finery in favor of homespun, ostracized the women who would not join in the protest. They also refused to serve tea, and instead drank coffee or cocoa or a tea substitute, an herb known as labradore, which was native to the area.

The merchant who was the strongest opponent of the boycott was a newcomer to Boston, John Mein, the printer and stationer who supplied stationery for the customs commissioners. He and his partner John Fleeming also published the Boston *Chronicle*, a newspaper they used to attempt to break the boycott by publishing the names of boycotting merchants continuing to import goods and claiming that the boycott was being used to gain unfair competition. He also distributed his newspaper to other colonial cities to try to convince them that Boston merchants were attempting to fool them.

By October Mein began to fear for his life,

Boston attorney James Otis, who with John Adams successfully defended a seaman who had resisted impressment into the British navy, had to defend his own life when he was attacked and seriously wounded by customs commissioner John Robinson.

and he and Fleeming started carrying pistols for protection. On the afternoon of October 28, they were walking in King Street when a group of other merchants approached them hurling insults. The two men drew their pistols and said they would shoot the first man to touch them. The group grew to a crowd of over a hundred, some estimate two hundred. When the crowd began to press in on them, Mein and Fleeming began to back away, seeking refuge at the Main Guard of the British troops. As Mein climbed up the steps to the Main Guard, one man swung a snow shovel at him and Fleeming fired his pistol, but no one was hit.

The crowd was unable to get at Mein and Fleeming, who were protected by the sentries standing watch outside the Main Guard, so it went through the streets rioting, attacking Mein's house, and accosting a seaman believed to be a British informer.

The boycott of British goods was originally intended to end on January 1, 1770, and most of the merchants, believing that it was working, wanted to continue it until England gave in to their demands. A few merchants began to defect, taking British goods out of storage and placing them on sale again.

In February the Sons of Liberty began posting signs saying "Importer," with accusing hands pointing toward the shops of merchants no longer participating in the boycott, and most citizens refused to patronize these establishments. Groups of young boys went further than this; they would occasionally pelt these merchants with dirt when they passed in the streets, and some broke a few shop windows.

On the night of February 21, a large group of boycotters tarred and feathered the windows of these shops, and the following morning they gathered in the street outside the store of the most vocal and persistent of their opponents, Theophilus Lillie, to bar the entrance to customers.

Lillie himself did nothing to try to remove the protesters. However, when no shoppers had tried to break through the crowd by noon, a neighbor, Ebenezer Richardson, decided to act. Richardson was a staunch royalist and a known customs informer. He first attempted to enlist assistance in breaking through the crowd to the shop door, but could persuade no one. He then commandeered a horse and wagon and attempted to force it through alone.

The crowd turned on him and began to pelt him with dirt, rocks, and sticks, forcing him to retreat to his house. He quickly came back out with a stick to try to club some of the mob, but he was again driven inside, this time returning with a musket loaded with buckshot, which he fired into the crowd.

Two young boys were wounded by the buckshot. One of them, eleven-year-old Christopher Snyder, was so badly injured he died a few hours later.

Church bells began to ring, calling the Sons of Liberty into the streets. Enraged by the injury of children, the mob captured Richardson and were ready to lynch him on the spot. However, the leaders of the Sons of Liberty persuaded them that Richardson had to be tried according to law, and they proceeded to take him to jail.

The funeral of Christopher Snyder was set for February 26, and the Sons of Liberty decided to turn the funeral procession into a demonstration against the British. Two days before the funeral, a massive snowstorm struck the city, one of those rare storms that not only covered the ground with a thick blanket of snow and ice but created an eerie atmosphere with lightning and thunder. Setting out from the Liberty Tree in the early evening, the funeral procession was almost a mile in length, beginning with over four hundred schoolboys walking in pairs. They were followed by the coffin, borne by six boys, with Snyder's family walking behind. After them came over two thousand mourners.

Eventually Richardson was tried for murder and found guilty by a colonial jury. However, the British appointed judges hesitated to sentence him to death, continually postponing a decision, in hopes local passions would subside.

They did not. For the colonists, hatred of the British government would only increase until a revolution was inevitable.

Crispus Attucks was in Boston at the time of Christopher Snyder's death, and as a member of the Sons of Liberty it is likely that he participated in the mob action outside Lillie's shop and in the subsequent funeral demonstration. He certainly participated in the events that followed.

The citizens of Boston were fed up with the British occupation of their city. The soldiers and the customs officials had to go. Almost everyone was now convinced that Samuel Adams and John Hancock were right: if England continued to treat them as subjects or slaves rather than as citizens with equal rights, then the colonies had to break free.

Young Snyder's death was the deciding factor for many people; they would submit to no more acts of tyranny by the representatives of the British government, whether military or civil. The next time there was a con-

frontation they would defy authority no matter what the consequences.

This does not appear to have been a decision made by the leaders of the Sons of
Liberty or by any other organized group. It
was merely talked about and passed on from
neighbor to neighbor, all of whom agreed to
take to the streets at the next sign of trouble. The signal would be the ringing of the
church bells, which was normally only the
call for volunteers to fight a fire.

For a few days after the Snyder funeral,
the weather remained extremely cold but
clear. Crispus Attucks, alias Michael
Johnson, was able to get work at the ropewalks for at least part of that time. On
Friday, March 2, Attucks was working with
the ropemakers and cablemakers laying rope
in John Gray's walks across from Commissioner Paxton's house between Pearl and
Congress streets, south of Milk street. The
plant was 744 feet long, and like most of the
other ropewalks it employed casual labor to
assist with the making of ropes and cables
for ships' rigging.

About midday, while they were working,
one of the off-duty British soldiers from the
Twenty-ninth Regiment, Patrick Walker,
came there to ask for work. All it took to set
off the tempers of the workmen was to see a

soldier in a red coat. One of the ropemakers, William Green, told him he could offer him work—cleaning his outhouse. (However, the language he used was a bit stronger.)

Walker responded to the insult by taking a swing at Green, and a fight quickly broke out. Outnumbered, Walker quickly left and returned with eight other soldiers to help him fight the ropemakers. Attucks eagerly joined in the fray, as did other workers, who came running from all over the ropewalks. The soldiers again retreated and returned with a larger number, estimated at about forty. This time it was Attucks who led the attack on the soldiers, and both sides were now armed, the soldiers carrying clubs and the ropemakers wielding the sticks they used for twining the rope.

Justice of the Peace John Hill had been watching the fracas from the window of his house, and now he called out to challenge Attucks, demanding to know what right a black man had to interfere in white men's quarrels. Surprised by the question, Attucks stepped out of the fracas momentarily but was quickly drawn back in.

Hill came outside and ordered the combatants to stop, which he had the right to do according to his office, but no one paid attention to him. Eventually the ropemakers drove the soldiers away, sending them running back to their barracks for more reinforcements. However, this time an officer managed to keep them from returning, and Justice Hill prevented the ropemakers from attacking the barracks.

Among the combatants were a colonist named Samuel Gray, a friend of Attucks', and a soldier named Matthew Kilroy. Both would continue to play parts in the events that were to follow, for the fight was not over: it was merely a temporary truce.

The following day there were several minor altercations as soldiers, individually and in small groups, attempted to seek revenge for their defeat. Three soldiers went to the ropewalks and attacked a group of three ropemakers, who were quickly joined by a sailor and a tanner. The soldiers were again driven off, one of them seriously injured.

Another soldier laid in wait for a ropemaker outside his rooming house but was beaten off by the ropemaker's landlord.

Naturally the British officers blamed the colonists for these "outrages" against soldiers of the Crown. That evening, a sergeant of the Twenty-ninth failed to return to barracks, and rumors spread that he had been killed by the ropemakers. His commanding officer, Lieutenant Colonel Maurice Carr, went to

Lieutenant Governor Thomas Hutchinson demanding something be done to protect the soldiers from the people.

On Sunday, the troops searched the rope-walks for the sergeant's body but turned up nothing to indicate foul play. A few hours later the sergeant arrived at his barracks with a hangover and the explanation that he had passed out in a Boston brothel.

Still, Lieutenant Governor Hutchinson spent much of Monday with his council trying to decide what could be done about the tense situation in Boston. Hutchinson wanted to achieve peace; the council insisted that the people would be satisfied with nothing less than removal of the troops from the city.

To make matters worse, there were unconfirmed rumors that there would be a major confrontation that evening between colonists and soldiers.

Meanwhile in London, unbenownst to anyone in Boston, Parliament, under pressure from British manufacturers and merchants suffering because of the colonial boycott of British goods, began to debate repeal of the Townshend Acts.

Chapter Seven.

The Boston Massacre

THE CLEAR WEATHER held throughout the day on Monday, March 5, though it remained intensely cold. The snow was still a foot deep in places, and the streets were slick with packed ice. Rumors spread among both townspeople and soldiers that there would be a confrontation that evening. The church bells would ring to call the people to gather in the streets to drive out the British troops, not just in Boston but in the surrounding towns, whose citizens would come to the city to assist.

No one knows how the rumors started, but

The British Grenadiers were the most hated of the troops in Boston because of their arrogance toward the citizens. They were also the most noticeable because of their tall bearskin hats.

it is clear that there was no definite or well-calculated plan by the Sons of Liberty, for when the citizens went into the streets, some armed themselves and some did not, and virtually none knew where the confrontation was to occur. They knew only to respond to the bells. And a great many people had not even heard the rumors, for when the bells began to ring they assumed it was for a fire. There are indications that these rumors were provoked by outright threats from soldiers, some of whom had been boasting that there were some Bostonians who would "not live to eat dinner on Tuesday."

Minor incidents continued to occur during the day as they had in the days before. One redcoat jabbed a citizen with the end of his rifle, but the man was not injured. In another incident a group of soldiers swaggered through Drapers' Alley, swinging their cutlasses at people, ripping their clothes. And groups of children roamed the streets throwing snowballs at off-duty soldiers.

As the day progressed the tension mounted. At sunset, people began to gather in small groups in the street, walking about and waiting for the signal that would bring the anticipated confrontation. Some carried sticks or clubs for protection.

The British troops went about their normal duties, with sentries posted at important positions around the city to protect government offices and officials. The permanent headquarters for the troops was the Main Guard, which had been situated in barracks south of the Town House on King Street.

King Street was the original name for what became State Street after the Revolution, and the Town House is what is now known as the "Old State House," situated in the middle of the street just before it dead-ends at Washington, then called "Marlborough" or "Cornhill." King Street branched around the Town House, with the north branch becoming Queen Street (now Court Street) after taking a jog across Cornhill. Even though it was relatively short, King Street was the principal east-west thoroughfare leading from the Long Wharf in the harbor to the government buildings, and therefore it had been laid out as very broad and open for heavy traffic.

West of the Town House, facing on Cornhill Street, was Old North Church. One block to the east was the Custom House, on the south side of King, at the corner of Royal Exchange Lane. Since one of the primary reasons the troops were in Boston was to enforce the collection of the customs taxes, the sentry placed in front of the Custom House was an

Boston in the 1770s was a thriving city, though it was hardly as peaceful as this 1776 drawing depicts. Not only the center of commerce and political life in New England, surrounded by

other important thriving towns, it was the home of rebellion and the revolutionary spirit, led by citizens such as Samuel Adams, John Hancock, James Otis, John Adams, and Dr. Joseph Warren.

important one. He was also a symbolic one
for the oppressed citizens and merchants of
Boston.

And it was with this sentry that the troubles began on the evening of March 5, 1770,
the trouble that would go down in history as
the Boston Massacre.

On duty at this sentry station that evening
was a young private named Hugh White, of
the Twenty-ninth Regiment, which had
taken over the watch from the Fourteenth at
noon. He was not easily visible to the two
sentries posted up the street in front of the
Main Guard because they were on the same
side of the street. It was also a rather dark
night, lit only by a quarter moon. (At this
time, Boston did not yet have streetlights.)

Upstairs at the Custom House lived the
family of Bartholomew Green, a minor customs official, and the family used both the
front and rear doors for access to their apart-
ment. One of Green's daughters, Ann, had
gone out shortly before eight o'clock to an
apothecary shop with a friend, Molly Rogers,
accompanied by a young man named
Bartholomew Broaders, who was an apprentice wigmaker.

The trouble in front of the Custom House
began with an associate of Broaders' named
Edward Garrick, who was apprenticed to the

The Old South Meeting House, at the corner of Washington and Milk streets, was one of the many churches in Boston to begin ringing its bells on the evening of March 5, 1770, calling the people from their homes.

same wigmaker. He was passing the Custom House at the same time as off-duty Lieutenant John Goldfinch of the Fourteenth Regiment. Goldfinch was one of the more arrogant and abusive of the British officers, hated by the colonists. There was a brief argument between Garrick and Goldfinch over the fact that the officer would not pay for wigs he had purchased from Garrick's employer.

Sentry Hugh White broke up the argument, instructing the two men to move on. Goldfinch did, but Garrick remained to argue with White and was still there when his friend Broaders returned with the two young ladies. Garrick told them of his dispute, and Broaders reported that they had just passed a group of men wielding clubs and claiming that a group of soldiers had attacked them.

As they were talking, Ann's brother Hammond came out of the Custom House and told the two young men, Broaders and Garrick, to come inside. They did but came back out shortly afterward to take a walk. It was about eight-thirty when they returned, and Garrick approached the sentry to resume the argument about the soldiers not paying their bills.

The argument grew heated, attracting the attention of a group of young boys. Finally

Hugh White lost control and struck Garrick across the face with his musket, drawing blood and knocking the apprentice wigmaker to the icy street. Quickly, two Green brothers, Hammond and John, came out of the Custom House and took Garrick and Broaders inside to treat Garrick's wound.

The group of young boys who had witnessed the incident began to taunt the sentry, throwing snowballs at him as well as calling him a "lobster" and a "bloodyback." The next few moments were chaotic. White, the sentry, attempted to ward off the pelting of snowballs, retreating to the front steps of the Custom House and trying to escape inside, but Hammond Green had locked the door. It is not known if White fought back against the boys, but one of them began to run down the street with blood on his face, crying out, "I'm killed! I'm killed!"

Unable to escape, White stood atop the small three-stepped portico of the Custom House and began to load his musket and affix his bayonet. He also began to shout to the sentries posted down the street in front of the Main Guard for assistance.

At about this time the church bells began to toll all over the city, and citizens everywhere took to the streets. Throughout Boston there were shouts of "Fire! Fire!"

King Street was the major thoroughfare in central Boston, leading from the docks to the Town House, seen above. It was wider than most streets and became a natural gathering place

for protesters because it contained not only the Town House but also the Custom House, occupied by the most hated of the representatives of the British Crown, the customs collectors.

Crispus Attucks heard the church bells while he was eating dinner at Thomas Symmonds' tavern on Cornhill, a short distance away from the Custom House. He hurriedly finished his meal and ran outside to see what was happening.

A crowd was already gathering in King Street in front of the Custom House, with men now joining the boys throwing snowballs and pieces of ice at White.

Sensing that this was to be the anticipated confrontation with the soldiers, Attucks hurried down to the docks to tell his friends. Gathering a group of about thirty or forty seamen and ropemakers, he led them back up King Street. In his group were Samuel Gray, the ropemaker whom Attucks had joined in the fight a few days before, and Robert Patterson, a seaman who had been in the mob when Richardson killed young Snyder and had been hit by some of the buckshot but not badly injured. Along the way they armed themselves with sticks and clubs. Attucks himself found a cordwood stick about four feet long and the thickness of a wrist. Others demolished an outdoor butcher's stand to take the wood for clubs.

At the Main Guard, Captain Thomas Preston, who was captain of the day, was faced with a difficult dilemma. His lieutenant, James Bassett, was not present, and it was up to him to decide what to do about the difficult situation down the street. One of his men was trapped on the steps of the Custom House, unable to move and threatened by a mob, but so far no harm had come to him. It was Preston's duty to go to White's aid, but if he took troops and attempted to force his way through the mob, the situation could grow worse and possibly result in bloodshed. And technically he did not have the authority to disperse a mob unless ordered to do so by civilian authority, such as a justice of the peace, or preferably the royal governor or lieutenant governor.

Preston paced up and down in front of the Main Guard trying to decide what to do.

Crowds were gathering in various parts of town, one of them in Dock Square. Over three hundred collected at the Liberty Tree. Another large group assembled before the Murray Barracks, where some of the troops were housed. At this location, a group of young boys were throwing snowballs at soldiers outside the barracks. A group of adults here advised Captain Goldfinch, whose unwillingness to pay his wig bill had started the trouble, to take the soldiers inside to avoid trouble. Goldfinch did, but as they retreated some in the crowd yelled,

"Cowards!"

And the bells kept ringing.

A young seaman named James Caldwell heard the pealing while he was at the home of a young lady he hoped to marry. He was not from Boston but like Attucks worked aboard a merchant vessel that was in port, yet he responded to the call of the bells and went out into the streets, eventually finding his way to the Custom House.

Seventeen-year-old Samuel Maverick, who was an apprentice ivory turner working for Isaac Greenwood, was having dinner with the family of Jonathon Cary when they heard the bells. After finishing their meal, Maverick joined Cary and his four sons to assist in fighting what they thought was a fire. They too were drawn to King Street.

Patrick Carr, who had recently immigrated from Ireland and worked for a maker of leather breeches, armed himself with a small cutlass on the way out of his employer's house, obviously aware of what the bells meant. However, his employer stopped him and took the cutlass away from him. Disarmed, Carr set out for the Custom House.

Seventeen-year-old Christopher Monk, known as "Kit," carried a catstick, a bat used in a form of stickball called "tip-cat," as he left his family's home and headed toward King Street.

Estimates of the number of people roaming the streets of Boston in groups range from one thousand to five thousand. It seems likely that there were well over a thousand, but not all of them were in King Street at this point. However, the mob there had grown to well over three hundred shortly after nine o'clock when Captain Preston made his decision to send a guard to assist White.

Lieutenant James Bassett had arrived from his quarters by this time, but he was of no use whatsoever, continually asking Preston what to do, so Preston himself called out a guard under Corporal William Wemms and ordered them to fall out in front of the Main Guard before proceeding down the street to the Custom House.

The six privates called out were all Royal Grenadiers, impressive because of their tall bearskin hats. They were William McCauley, Matthew Kilroy, Hugh Montgomery, William Warren, John Carroll, and James Hartigan. Unfortunately, three of these men had been among the soldiers involved in the ropewalks brawl with Attucks, Gray, and the ropemakers on the preceding Friday.

With Corporal Wemms in the lead and

with Captain Preston following, the guard set off down King Street in double files, holding their muskets in diagonal position so that— it was hoped—the demonstrators would move out of the way to avoid being pricked by the bayonets. However, the throng was so thick that there were several unavoidable minor brushes, with curses from citizens and angry responses from Wemms commanding people to move out of the way.

When they arrived at the Custom House, Wemms ordered his men to halt and load their muskets, a complicated procedure requiring them to place the weapons' butts on the ground and then to pour powder into the barrels before stuffing a ball inside.

From the very beginning of the trouble, bookseller Henry Knox had been trying to calm the crowd and establish peace. The sight of the guard loading their muskets now upset him, and he grabbed Preston by the arm and shouted, "For God's sake, take care of your men. If they fire, you die."

"I am sensible of it," Preston replied, rather annoyed.

Preston ordered the terrified Private White to fall in, which he did without interference from the crowd. However, when they attempted to march back to the Main Guard, the crowd would not permit the soldiers to move but pressed in more closely.

Some in the mob shouted challenges to the British to fire. Preston shouted back at the people, ordering them to disperse. Some threw snowballs at him. Justice of the Peace James Murray arrived at this point to read the Riot Act, which would require the mob to leave, but the mob forced him away before he could perform his duty.

The church bells continued to toll ominously. The shouts of "Fire!" from the crowd, which had now grown to over four hundred, increased as Preston tried to reestablish order among the guard, setting them up in a line extending outward into the street from the walk in front of the Custom House. Preston stood in front of the men, with White positioned between them. At the south end of the irregular line was Corporal Wemms, with the grenadiers lined up to his left in this order: Hartigan, Warren, McCauley, Carroll, Kilroy, and Montgomery at the outside vulnerable position.

Crispus Attucks was at the front of the crowd only a few feet from Montgomery, with his friend Samuel Gray by his side. James Caldwell was a bit farther back, out in the street. Attucks and Gray confronted two of the men they had fought at the ropewalks—Montgomery and Kilroy. In fact, Kilroy had been the man Gray had personally beaten off that day.

It was clear that the two grenadiers wanted to get their revenge, and angry words passed between them and Attucks and Gray. From what happened next, it seems likely that Attucks and Gray were among the people challenging the soldiers to fire.

Attucks reached out and grabbed the barrel of Montgomery's musket, then swung his stick at the soldier. Montgomery fell on his backside, with his gun clattering to the ice beside him. As he struggled to his feet, he yelled to his compatriots, "Damn you, fire!" Then he fired the first shot wildly, which struck Attucks in the chest but not killing him.

With the realization that he was hit, Attucks leaned on his stick for support. Then a second shot from Montgomery struck him in the chest, this one felling him, causing him to collapse to the ice, dead.

Matthew Kilroy fired next, his shot hitting Samuel Gray in the head, killing him instantly. At the time he was shot, Gray was standing with his hands in his pockets.

Even though neither Corporal Wemms nor Captain Preston had ordered their men to fire, a barrage of shots now rang out. The crowd began to run, attempting to escape, some rushing down King Street, others around the corner into Exchange Lane. However, a few people stood their ground and engaged in hand-to-hand combat with the guard, preventing them from firing.

Young Samuel Maverick was one of those running away when he was hit by a bullet and fell to the street, seriously injured. Two bullets struck James Caldwell, killing him.

Patrick Carr was on the other side of the street when he was hit, not killed but critically injured, with the musket ball having struck him in the hip, taking away part of his spine.

Six others were injured, among them young Christopher Monk; Edward Payne, who was struck in the arm while standing in the doorway of his home; Robert Patterson, who took a musket ball in his wrist; and Nathaniel Fosdick, who was stabbed with a bayonet.

After the first volley, the guard had to stop to reload their muskets. Only then did Captain Preston manage to regain command and order the men to stop firing.

One of the citizens in the crowd, Benjamin Burdick, bent down to Attucks' body and confirmed that he was dead. He then stood up again, walked over to Preston, stared him in the face, and stated, "I want to see some faces

The Boston Massacre is depicted above in the famous print by Paul Revere, published in his broadside just after the event. Though rather crude, it gives the only contemporary "likenesses"

Within the image: BUTCHER'S HALL

Printed & Sold by Paul Revere

of the victims. The figure in the foreground with the dog at his feet is considered to be Crispus Attucks. The man on the ground at center, bleeding from the head, is clearly Samuel Gray.

that I may swear to another day." It was a clear statement that the citizens intended to see the British troops tried in a court of law.

And Preston clearly understood. He replied, "Perhaps, sir, you may."

The officer was then permitted to march his guard back to the barracks at the Main Guard, as the colonists began to look to the dead and injured. However, as they departed, Private Matthew Kilroy paused to stab his bayonet into Samuel Gray's shattered skull.

With the violence over, the crowd in King Street grew to over a thousand as people were drawn to see the scene of the tragedy. At the barracks, Captain Preston called out the rest of the regiment and placed them in street firing position in case the enraged mob should attempt to attack.

Although many continued to harangue the soldiers, most were suffering from shock at what had taken place.

The body of Samuel Gray was carried to a doctor's house on Cornhill Street, but the doctor wasn't home, so the body was left on the doorstep. The badly injured Samuel Maverick was taken to his mother's boarding house on Union Street, where he died. James Caldwell's body was carried to the prison house.

Patrick Carr, who was injured but still alive, was taken to a house in Fitch's Alley, while someone went for a doctor. He was tended by a loyalist physician, Dr. John Jeffries. Later Carr was returned to the home of his employer. Despite medical efforts to save him, he eventually died of his wounds.

The body of Crispus Attucks was taken to the Royal Exchange Tavern in Exchange Lane, around the corner from where he was killed. It was only after his death that one of his friends revealed that Michael Johnson was not his true name, that he was in fact Crispus Attucks, who had escaped from slavery in Framingham twenty years before.

The 29th Regiment have already left us, and the 14th Regiment are following them, so that we expect the Town will soon be clear of all the Troops. The Wisdom and true Policy of his Majesty's Council and Col. Dalrymple the Commander appear in this Measure. Two Regiments in the midst of this populous City; and the Inhabitants justly incensed: Those of the neighbouring Towns actually under Arms upon the first Report of the Massacre, and the Signal only wanting to bring in a few Hours to the Gates of this City many Thousands of our brave Brethren in the Country, deeply affected with our Distresses, and to whom we are greatly obliged on this Occasion—No one knows where this would have ended, and what important Consequences even to the whole British Empire might have followed, which our Moderation and Loyalty upon so trying an Occasion, and our Faith in the Commander's Assurances have happily prevented.

Last Thursday, agreeable to a general Request of the Inhabitants, and by the Consent of Parents and Friends, were carried to their Grave in Succession, the Bodies of *Samuel Gray*, *Samuel Maverick*, *James Caldwell*, and *Crispus Attucks*, the unhappy Victims who fell in the bloody Massacre of the day Evening preceding!

On this Occasion most of the Shops in Town were shut, all the Bells were ordered to toll a solemn Peal, as were also those in the neighboring Towns of Charlestown Roxbury, &c. The Procession began to move between the Hours of 4 and 5 in the Afternoon; two of the unfortunate Sufferers, viz. Mess. *James Caldwell* and *Crispus Attucks*, who were Strangers, borne from Faneuil-Hall, attended by a numerous Train of Persons of all Ranks; and the other two, viz. Mr. *Samuel Gray*, from the House of Mr. Benjamin Gray, (his Brother) on the North-side the Exchange, and Mr. *Maverick*, from the House of his distressed Mother Mrs. *Mary Maverick*, in Union-Street, each followed by their respective Relations and Friends: The several Hearses forming a Junction in King-Street, the Theatre of that inhuman Tragedy! proceeded from thence thro' the Main-Street, lengthened by an immense Concourse of People, so numerous as to be obliged to follow in Ranks of six, and brought up by a long Train of Carriages belonging to the principal Gentry of the Town. The Bodies were deposited in one Vault in the middle Burying-ground: The aggravated Circumstances of their Death, the Distress and Sorrow visible in every Countenance, together with the peculiar Solemnity with which the whole Funeral was conducted, surpass Description.

Chapter Eight

Rallying 'round the Martyrs

To THE CITIZENS of Boston on the day after the massacre in King Street, it did not matter that Crispus Attucks was black, nor did it concern them that he had been a slave twenty years before. What mattered was that he and three other human beings had been killed by the soldiers occupying their city. (Another, Patrick Carr, still clung to life, though he had virtually no chance of surviving.)

Early that Tuesday morning, four thousand people responded to the call of Samuel Adams for a town meeting at Faneuil Hall,

The obituary of the Boston Massacre victims printed by Paul Revere has preserved not only a description of the events of the day but also the passionate feelings of the people of Boston.

in which to demand that Lieutenant Governor Thomas Hutchinson order the British troops to leave Boston "or face serious consequences." The meeting gave Adams the vote he wanted and appointed him, John Hancock, William Molineux, and Deacon William Phillips as a committee to call upon Hutchinson and present their demand.

While this was taking place, Hutchinson was in a council meeting he had called at the Town House, hoping to enlist the aid of the councilors in calming the tense situation. The Lieutenant Governor had had only about three hours sleep. After the shooting the night before, the city had come very close to a full-scale rebellion. Once the bodies had been removed from the street, the crowd had regrouped and surrounded the Town House, demanding Hutchinson order the troops to leave the city.

Citizens from the surrounding towns had been called out, arming themselves and preparing to march to the aid of Boston, waiting only for the signal of a fire at the top of Beacon Hill. The barrel of pitch for the fire was already there, and men stood by to light it if another fight should break out.

Although the offending soldiers had returned to their barracks, Lieutenant Colonel William Dalrymple and Lieutenant

Samuel Adams was the acknowledged leader of the revolutionary group of colonists known as the "Sons of Liberty" long before the massacre, but he gained an even greater following during and after the trial of the British soldiers.

Colonel Maurice Carr had ordered other troops into the streets near the crowd "to maintain order." However, to the citizens in the streets the mere presence of the military was provocation and entirely "out of order."

The situation was even more volatile than it had been earlier.

Hutchinson stepped out on the second floor balcony overlooking King Street and addressed the people. As he had done from the moment the soldiers had arrived, the Lieutenant Governor insisted that he did not have the power to give "orders" to the troops. However, he promised to investigate the actions of the military in this case and see that any soldiers or officers guilty of breaking the law would be punished. "The law shall have its course," he said. "I will live and die by the law."

The crowd yelled back to him that they would not disperse until the soldiers had returned to their barracks.

Hutchinson was in a very delicate position. If he "ordered" the soldiers to leave, it would be acknowledgment that he had possessed the power to give them orders all along— including the order to leave Boston. Hutchinson left the balcony and went to the south window, beneath which Lieutenant Colonel Carr had positioned his men; there

Lieutenant Governor Thomas Hutchinson, later to become Governor, attempted to mediate between the citizens of Boston and the British military in the city, constantly protesting to the people that he had no authority over the troops.

he called down to Carr, "requesting" that he remove the troops, telling him that the crowd was willing to disperse once the soldiers were in their barracks.

It is not known whether Carr interpreted this as a "request" or an "order," but he removed his men, and soon afterward the citizens returned to their homes.

Hutchinson proceeded to work far into the night. Assisted by two justices of the peace, Richard Dana and John Tudor, he began his investigation of the actions of the soldiers to determine whether they should be arrested and brought before a grand jury. He called as many witnesses as could be identified who had been near enough to the scene to have seen and heard what took place. Some had to be roused from their beds.

The witnesses did not agree whether Captain Thomas Preston had given an order to his men to fire. Some swore they had only heard him shout, "For God's sake, do not fire!" Others swore they had heard him voice the word "fire" but could not be sure if it was an order or part of a longer command.

By two o'clock in the morning, Lieutenant Governor Hutchinson decided there was sufficient evidence of "probable cause" to bring the matter before a grand jury. He had the sheriff issue warrants for the arrest of the officers and men involved. Lieutenant Bassett, was found first and brought in, but he was released. Captain Preston could not be found, and for awhile it appeared that he had fled to escape prosecution, but by three o'clock he was located, arrested, and placed in jail.

A few hours later the other eight soldiers surrendered and were placed under arrest.

Before going to bed for a short nap, Hutchinson arranged for Dr. Benjamin Church to perform an autopsy on the body of Crispus Attucks at the Royal Exchange Tavern and for county coroners Robert Pierpoint and Thomas Crafts to prepare an inquest on the four victims.

To his credit, the Lieutenant Governor was doing his best to live up to his promise to "live or die" by the law. But he remained in a very precarious position, for he persisted in maintaining he had no authority to give orders to the military; only General Thomas Gage in New York had the authority to remove the troops from the city.

When Samuel Adams and his committee appeared before Hutchinson and the councilors at the Town House on Tuesday morning, conveying the citizens' demands that the troops leave Boston, Hutchinson held his position staunchly. However, Lieutenant

Colonel Dalrymple, seeking a compromise, offered to remove the Twenty-ninth Regiment, which the citizens considered to be the most "obnoxious," to their original posting of Castle William.

The shrewd Sam Adams argued that, if they had the authority to remove one regiment, they had the authority to remove both the Twenty-ninth and the Fourteenth, releasing the city from martial law entirely. Nevertheless, the committee returned to the citizens at Faneuil Hall with the offer. By this time the town meeting had grown so large that the thousands of people had to move to the Old South Church.

They voted almost unanimously to reject the offer. When Adams and his committee went back to Hutchinson to report the vote of the town meeting, they took with them representatives from other towns around to verify that, if all the troops were not removed from the colony, there were ten thousand citizens armed and ready for a full rebellion against the Crown. With this the Council, led by Royall Tyler, sided with the colonists and against Hutchinson, insisting that all the troops had to be removed. They argued that the Lieutenant Governor could follow the same course he had the night before: he could "request" that they leave, and if the officers

After the massacre in King Street, some of the troops were removed from Boston to Castle William, an island fortress in Boston Harbor, seen here in the background flying the British flag, with a British ship in the foreground.

followed his wishes it was their decision.

Since the officers and Hutchinson's advisors agreed with this course, the Lieutenant Governor stood entirely alone. He finally gave in; both regiments would withdraw to Castle William while informing General Gage of the situation and requesting orders. The citizens of Boston had won a victory.

However, the regiments were not quick to fulfill the promise. When the officers and men of the Twenty-ninth and the Fourteenth learned of the decision, they were incensed at having to depart in disgrace. Some of the officers argued for remaining in Boston while awaiting General Gage's orders.

The military presence was still very much in evidence on Thursday, March 8, the day set for the funeral of the four victims of the massacre. The weather was still cold and clear as the mourners assembled, some coming in from out of town, some expressing genuine grief, others participating in the funeral as a sign of defiance against the British.

Two of the victims were Bostonians, and they had relatives and friends to mourn. Samuel Gray's body lay at the house of his brother, Benjamin Gray, on the north side of the Royal Exchange Lane, where the family accepted condolence calls. Samuel Maverick's body lay at the home of his mother, Mrs.

Mary Maverick, in Union Street, where relatives and friends came to call.

The other two, Crispus Attucks and James Caldwell, had no homes or relatives in Boston, so their bodies were placed in Faneuil Hall. Here the largest group, those who had come to rally for freedom rather than to grieve, gathered for the ceremonies. There were people from all walks of life in attendance, from seamen and crafts apprentices to merchants and lawyers and even the gentry and first families of Boston.

Shortly after four o'clock in the afternoon, the four coffins were taken from their viewing places and loaded onto separate horse-drawn hearses draped in black. For a short distance there were three separate funeral processions, but in King Street, at the site of the massacre, they joined into one massive procession of twelve thousand people.

As they set out together, the hearses led the way. They were followed by the masses of people, walking in ranks of six abreast; and behind them came the carriages of the gentry and town leaders, in full force, for the first time showing the King and Parliament that, if tyranny persisted, they would have to contend with *all* the colonists.

Or at least almost all. There were still loyalists in Boston, and some of them, along

Faneuil Hall, later to be noted for the anti-slavery meetings of the abolition movement, was the scene of citizens' meetings protesting the British laws and the presence of troops in Boston

prior to the Revolution. On the day of the funeral of the victims, two of the bodies—those of Crispus Attucks and James Caldwell—rested there before being taken for burial.

with some of the British soldiers, came out to watch the funeral procession. One loyalist, a clergyman named Mather Byles, commented to a friend as he watched the cortege pass: "They call me a brainless Tory. But tell me, my young friend, which is better: to be ruled by one tyrant three thousand miles away or by three thousand tyrants not one mile away?"

The procession did not go directly to the cemetery but first made a symbolic trip to the Liberty Tree. It was an impressive assemblage, extending as it did for many blocks. From the Liberty Tree, the cortege proceeded to the Old Granary Burying Ground, where a single vault had been prepared for the four coffins in the middle part of the cemetery.

It was impossible for all of the mourners to participate in the graveside service, so the family and friends and some of the dignitaries were given place beside the vault. The service was respectful, simple, and brief; although the procession had been a demonstration of defiance, the burial was solemn.

Nine days later, on Saturday, March 17, the vault was reopened and there was another funeral procession, as the fifth victim, Patrick Carr, was laid to rest alongside the other four. Again the citizens of Boston came

A British cartoon depicted colonists forcing tea down the throat of a tarred-and feathered England with the Boston Tea Party. In the background can be seen not only colonists tossing tea off a ship but also the Liberty Tree with a noose hanging from a limb.

out in force.

The shocking and senseless violence of the massacre in King Street united the people of Massachusetts against the Crown as no earlier British outrage had done. The upper and middle classes could no longer sit back comfortably and ignore what was happening. And it was not just New England that was affected by the massacre. As the news spread throughout the British colonies—New York, Pennsylvania, Virginia, South Carolina, and the others—the injustice was added to all of those they had felt locally at the hands of the British.

Paul Revere printed an engraving of the massacre in King Street, accompanied by a poem:

Unhappy Boston! see thy Sons deplore,
Thy hallow'd Walks besmear'd with guiltless
    Gore,
While faithless P[resto]n and his savage
    Bands,
With murd'rous Rancour stretch their bloody
    Hands;
Like fierce Barbarians grinning o'er their
    Prey,
Approve the Carnage and enjoy the Day.

If scalding drops from Rage from Anguish
    Wrung,
If speechless Sorrows lab'ring for a Tongue,

Or if a weeping World can ought appease
The plaintive Ghosts of Victims such as
  these;
The Patriot's copious Tears for each are shed,
A glorious Tribute which embalms the Dead.

But know Fate summons to that awful Goal,
Where Justice strips the Murd'rer of his
  Soul;
Should venal C[our]ts the scandal of the
  land,
Snatch the relentless Villain from her Hand,
Keen Execrations on this Plate inscrib'd,
Shall reach a Judge who never can be brib'd.

By the time of Carr's funeral, the British troops had withdrawn to Castle William, though not without continual pressure from the citizens, including increasing threats from Samuel Adams, who finally had to inform Lieutenant Governor Hutchinson that, if he did not live up to his promise, the people would take action against him personally. On March 10, the Twenty-ninth Regiment departed for Castle William, and the Fourteenth the following day. The orders from General Gage for the troops to remain in Boston arrived too late; once they were out of the city, the Sons of Liberty were patrolling the streets and nine men were in jail awaiting a civil trial.

Chapter Nine

John Adams
for the Defense

HISTORIANS HAVE made much of the fact that John Adams undertook the defense of the British soldiers when they were brought to trial for killing the citizens in the Boston Massacre. Adams, later the great patriot and the second president of the United States, was politically a moderate at the time. Along with most of the citizens of Boston, he opposed the abuses by the British Crown and Parliament, but he did not favor a break from British rule as did his cousin Samuel Adams.

When he was asked to take on the case,

Despite his personal sentiments, John Adams agreed to defend the British soldiers in the civil trial because he believed that every man deserved a fair hearing before the court.

John Adams was reluctant, but he was convinced by the argument that the soldiers could not get a fair trial if he did not accept. The fact that his sympathies lay with the citizens of Boston rather than with the soldiers was considered an advantage. The same argument was used in persuading Josiah Quincy, Jr., to join the defense. At the time, John Adams was thirty-four years old and Quincy was twenty-six. The third counselor on the team, Robert Auchmuty, was a loyalist and considerably older.

Interestingly, the solicitor general who would be prosecuting the case was Josiah Quincy's older brother, Samuel Quincy, who was one of John Adams' best friends and a loyalist whose sympathies lay with the soldiers rather than the citizens. To offer some balance to the prosecution, the radical citizens, led by Sam Adams, pressured to have a more sympathetic attorney appointed to assist. The Crown was very sensitive to criticism at this point, so Robert Treat Paine was added to the prosecution.

John Adams realized from the outset that this would be a very difficult case to defend, especially since he would be representing not only Captain Thomas Preston but also the other eight soldiers involved. The defenses he could plead for his clients were rather limit-

Josiah Quincy, Jr., assisted John Adams in defending the British soldiers. At age twenty-six, he was considerably younger than Adams, and his zealousness in preparing the case led him to serious disagreements with the senior counselor.

ed. The best defense for Preston would be that he had not issued the order to fire, but that would mean the soldiers were guilty of acting without orders; their best defense would be that they were merely obeying the officer's command. The only other defense would be that all had acted in self-defense, but that would mean that Adams would have to prove that the citizens of Boston were guilty of mob violence.

Despite his own sympathies, this was what Adams was forced to do.

An added problem was that, from the outset, the case was already being tried in the press and in the public houses, both in the colonies and in England: the colonists had already found the soldiers guilty, and the British people had acquitted them even before the court trial began. In Boston there were threats that, if Preston was acquitted by a jury, he would be captured by the mob and hanged.

In the days immediately after the massacre, passions remained high; the citizens of Boston wanted blood. For this reason, they demanded the trial be held immediately. Adams and the other defense attorneys preferred a delay to allow tempers to cool, which would increase their chances of getting a fair jury.

After the soldiers were indicted on March 13, the judges scheduled the trial for June. However, Sam Adams and a group of citizens marched into the courtroom and demanded that the cases be tried immediately. Intimidated, the judges set a date in April.

Unfortunately, the judges' bench suffered a series of illnesses and accidents that made postponing the trial a necessity. Under the British system, cases normally were heard by a panel of five judges; at least two were absolutely essential. The Chief Justice of the Massachusetts court was Thomas Hutchinson, who had recently been raised from Lieutenant Governor to Governor of the colony. He could not sit because he was personally involved in the case.

The prisoners were finally arraigned on September 7, and the trial set for late October. Meanwhile, the news arrived in Boston that Parliament had repealed the Townshend Acts, except for the tax on tea. Under the circumstances, this news did little to calm the colonists' opposition to the British Crown.

By the time the court was ready to hear the case, beginning on October 24, it had decided that Captain Preston should be tried separately from his men. Preston's case was to be heard first, and four judges would sit on the bench—Edmund Trowbridge, Peter Oliver, John Cushing, and Benjamin Lynde serving as Chief Justice.

Under normal circumstances in the colonial courts, even criminal cases did not last more than a day. At the outset everyone was aware that these cases would be an exception; they would be lucky if they were able to impanel a jury in one day. As it turned out, they took even longer than anticipated; the trial of Captain Preston took six days (seven including Sunday), and that of the men took eight (nine including Sunday). The juries had to be housed and fed during that time to keep them from being contaminated by contact with the community.

With Preston's trial, the precaution was hardly necessary. Unable to gather an impartial jury, the prosecution was forced to accept five jurors who were prejudiced in the defendant's favor. Since Preston was being tried for murder, a capital offense, the jury decision would have to be unanimous. From the beginning there were only two possible outcomes—acquittal or a divided jury, the latter requiring that the case be retried.

As it turned out, the prosecution's case was very weak. Samuel Quincy and Robert Paine had to prove beyond a reasonable doubt that Captain Thomas Preston had ordered his

The man chosen to be the chief prosecuting attorney in the case against the British soldiers was Samuel Quincy, brother of Josiah Quincy, one of the defense attorneys. His sympathies were for the soldiers rather than the people of Boston.

men to fire on the crowd in King Street. Most of their witnesses came off as confused or contradictory. The most credible testified that the man they heard give the command to fire was wearing an overcoat; on cross-examination, John Adams was able to prove that Preston had not been wearing one.

Near the end of the second day, the prosecution concluded its case and Adams was able to make the opening presentation for the defense. However, it was on the third day that he brought on his two best witnesses. One was Richard Palmes, a member of the Sons of Liberty, who had been standing arguing with Captain Preston. Palmes had been the closest man to the officer when the violence had broken out. Not only did he swear that Preston had not issued the command, Palmes admitted that he himself had been wearing a cloth overcoat that fit the description given by other witnesses.

The second key defense witness was a black man, Andrew, the slave of Oliver Wendell (grandfather of the noted writer and great-grandfather of the Supreme Court Justice). Like Palmes, Andrew had been participating in the demonstration against the soldiers, and he admitted that he had thrown pieces of ice at the redcoats. However, the most important aspect of Andrew's testimo-

In order to have at least one of the prosecuting attorneys sympathetic toward the people, Robert Treat Paine was appointed to assist Samuel Quincy in the case against the British soldiers.

ny was that he was able to describe the actions of Crispus Attucks in the fray. He testified that Attucks had come striding up to the soldiers, leading a group of men wielding sticks, and that Attucks had attempted to strike Preston with his stick and then had struck at Montgomery.

Aware that the testimony of a black man, especially a slave, would be doubted, Adams brought Oliver Wendell to the stand to swear that Andrew was of good character and had never been known to lie.

The case was going very much in favor of the defense. However, before the third day was over, a dispute arose between John Adams and his co-counsel, Josiah Quincy, which almost stopped the trial. Quincy wanted to bring on more witnesses to testify to the mob atmosphere that prevailed among the citizens in King Street; Adams was determined to tread a fine line to keep from indicting the citizens of Boston for creating a riot. Only when Adams threatened to withdraw from the case did Quincy give in.

The case was finally handed over to the jury at the end of the fifth day, and they reported their verdict the following morning, Tuesday, October 30, which happened to be John Adams' thirty-fifth birthday. Captain Thomas Preston was not guilty; he was

A panel of four judges sat for the trials of Captain Preston and the British soldiers, headed by Benjamin Lynde (above) as chief justice. The others were Peter Oliver, Edmund Trowbridge, and John Cushing.

removed from jail and taken to Castle William for his own safety.

With Preston acquitted, there was added pressure on both sides for the second trial, that of the eight men who had been under Preston's command in King Street—Corporal William Wemms and Privates James Hartigan, William McCauley, Hugh White, Mathew Kilroy, William Warren, John Carroll, and Hugh Montgomery. Not only was the public crying for blood, but the "not guilty" verdict for Preston made Adams' task in defending the men more difficult. If the prosecution could prove that any or all of the men had fired their weapons, the only plea open to him was self-defense. This time, Adams would be senior defense counsel, as Auchmuty would not be participating.

The trial of *Rex v. Wemms et al.* began on Tuesday, November 27. It was even more difficult than before to find an impartial jury. They were able to impanel only nine jurors from the pool that had been called, then had to resort (as they had in the first trial) to pulling in men from the street, which was the procedure followed under British law. When they finally had a complete jury, none of its members were from Boston.

There was one major procedural difference between this trial and Preston's. The prosecution asked the court for permission to admit testimony showing that the British troops had made threats against the citizens before the events in King Street. This was not normally permitted under British law, and the judges were reluctant to allow it. However, Adams agreed to this procedure if the defense would be permitted to introduce evidence showing that the citizens had threatened the soldiers.

It proved to be a shrewd move by Adams, especially when it turned out that the prosecution was as ill-prepared as it had been in the first trial. Because of their confusing testimony as to what precisely had taken place in King Street, most prosecution witnesses were not very credible. One very embarrassing moment occurred when a witness took the stand and testified that he had not been in King Street, but that the person they wanted was his brother. What made it worse was that John Adams and Josiah Quincy were often able to turn the prosecution witnesses around on cross-examination to make points for the defense.

In cross-examining a sailor who was a prosecution witness, Quincy got him to admit that he had witnessed Crispus Attucks wielding a stick and leading a large crowd on its way to King Street and that he had seen a "stout man," presumably Attucks, strike Montgomery on the arm before Montgomery had fired his rifle.

Richard Palmes, who had been a defense witness in the first trial (the man in the overcoat standing next to Preston), was brought on to try to soften the sailor's testimony. Palmes stated that Montgomery had not fallen until after he had fired, and then he (Palmes) had been the one to strike the blow that sent Montgomery to the ground. The confusion that ensued hindered rather than helped the prosecution's case.

Adams and Quincy managed to get several more prosecution witnesses to admit on cross-examination that they had seen Attucks not only leading an armed group but striking the critical blow at Montgomery.

The prosecution used the court's special dispensation to bring on witnesses who testified about the ropewalk incident and several other altercations that had taken place before the massacre to show that the soldiers had provoked the citizens, but this did little to help the case for the Crown. They also called one witness who stated that he had heard Private Kilroy threaten to shoot townspeople if given the chance.

However, the strongest prosecution witnesses were two men, Joseph Crosswell and

One of the strongest defense witnesses was Dr. John Jeffries,
who had treated Patrick Carr after the shooting and testified that
Carr did not blame the soldiers for what they had done.

James Carter, who testified that they had seen blood on Kilroy's bayonet after the shooting, indicating that he had at least stabbed one of the victims.

Again, on the third day of trial, Adams came to loggerheads with his co-counsel Josiah Quincy, and it was for the same reason as in the Preston trial. As Quincy began the case for the defense, he took advantage of the court's special dispensation to call numerous witnesses to recount incidents of citizens provoking the soldiers prior to the shooting in King Street. Again Adams threatened to withdraw from the defense if Quincy did not cease attempts to show the citizenry in a negative light; again Quincy gave in.

The testimony for the defense on the fourth and fifth days proved to be the most important, for much of it pertained to the direct threats against the soldiers in King Street. On Friday, November 30, Patrick Keeton testified to meeting Attucks and his group on their way to King Street and witnessing the mulatto reaching into a woodpile and taking out two sturdy sticks, offering one of them to him. Keeton had joined the group and gave evidence that, after they arrived in King Street, Attucks had threatened the soldiers with his stick, cursing and swearing at them.

Later that same day, the defense brought

on its star witness, the slave Andrew, who testified as he had at Preston's trial to the fact that Attucks had provoked the soldiers, striking at Montgomery and scuffling with him. Andrew also stated that he had engaged in the provocation himself by throwing ice at the grenadiers. Again, Oliver Wendell, was brought to the stand to testify that Andrew was honest and truthful.

The next day, Patrick Carr's landlady and another person were called to testify that they had witnessed Carr attempt to take a sword with him when he had left his rooms to go into the street. And Dr. John Jeffries, who had treated Carr's wounds after the shooting, testified that Carr had confessed before he died to having provoked the soldiers to violence.

The summation and arguments by the attorneys for the two sides took two and a half days, beginning on Monday, December 3. In his argument for the defense, John Adams emphasized to the jury: "It is of more importance to the community that innocence should be protected than it is that guilt should be punished." However, in hopes of proving self-defense, he also tried to mitigate the actions of the soldiers by denigrating the character of the citizens who had attacked them, describing them as "a motley rabble of saucy boys, negroes and molattoes, Irish teagues and outlandish jack tars.... Why we should scruple to call such a set of people a mob, I cannot conceive, unless the name is too respectable for them." He also singled out the "stout Molatto fellow" as the ringleader of the mob, counting on prejudice against African Americans to influence the jury.

It is perhaps this characterization (or character assassination) of Crispus Attucks, utilized by Adams in aid of his clients, that has persisted among those historians who wish to minimize Attucks' place in history. Yet Adams himself recognized the importance of Attucks and the other martyrs of the Boston Massacre, for years later he would state, time and again, that the true date for the beginning of the American Revolution was March 5, 1770, with the events in King Street.

Early in the afternoon of December 5, the jury was permitted to withdraw for deliberation. At four o'clock it returned with its verdict. It found all eight of the defendants not guilty of murder, but with two it gave verdicts of "guilty of manslaughter"—Mathew Kilroy and Hugh Montgomery, the only two who had been proved to have fired their weapons. Wemms, Hartigan, McCauley, White, Warren, and Carroll were released and permitted to go in peace. Kilroy and

Montgomery were returned to jail to await sentencing, with little doubt that the sentence would be death.

However, under British law, as Christians, they had a way out, and they took it. When they were brought into court for sentencing on December 14, the judge asked if there was a reason why sentence of death should not be passed on them. They both "prayed benefit of clergy" by reading a verse from the Bible and extended their thumbs for branding.

This British tradition had existed since earliest Christian times. Essentially, it meant that anyone who could prove himself a Christian by reading the Bible could escape a death sentence. Christians would be punished by branding on the thumb. The death sentence was only for heathens.

Although Governor Hutchinson had been pressured to grant leniency and not even to inflict this punishment, he ordered the sheriff to carry out the branding, after which the prisoners were released.

Chapter Ten

The American Revolution

FOR A TIME, CALM was restored in Boston, but the people did not forget the massacre, and their attitude toward Britain did not improve. Even though Parliament had rescinded the Townshend Acts on April 12, 1770, it left the tax on tea and continued to deny that colonists had the same rights as British citizens. As long as the tea tax remained, so did the colonists' tea embargo. Some of the people opposed to the tax continued to drink tea, but only if they could get it smuggled into the colonies from

In composing the Declaration of Independence, Benjamin Franklin, Thomas Jefferson, and John Adams, seen here with Robert Livingston and Roger Sherman, sought to outlaw slavery.

other countries to avoid the tax. Otherwise they drank one of the tea substitutes.

Although there were no major confrontations between the colonists and the Crown for over a year after the Boston Massacre, the hostility continued on both sides. Hutchinson, now the Royal governor of Massachusetts, waged a lengthy fight with Sam and John Adams over his right to move the people's elected legislature to Cambridge from Boston, where he felt it was "contaminated" by radical ideas.

And in England, the British East India Tea Company was on the verge of bankruptcy as a result of the colonial tea embargo. Finally, to attempt to save the company, Parliament passed the Tea Act, removing the duty from tea imported into Britain but retaining it in the colonies.

On the night of December 16, 1773, three British ships lay at anchor in Boston Harbor, their holds filled with British tea—eighteen thousand British pounds worth. The men of Boston, many of whom had been in King Street on the night of the Boston Massacre, were determined to show King George and Parliament that they were no longer willing to submit to injustice. As an act of defiance, they devised the Boston Tea Party. Dressing like Mohawk Indians, they boarded the three ships—the *Dartmouth*, the *Eleanor*, and the *Beaver*—and tossed the precious cargo overboard into the harbor.

From that point the hostilities between the colonies and the mother country began to escalate. Three months after the Boston Tea Party, Parliament passed four bills, known collectively as the "Intolerable Acts," specifically to punish the people of Massachusetts. The first closed the port of Boston until the people had paid for the tea that had been destroyed; the second prohibited public meetings in Massachusetts unless approved by the governor; the third prohibited the colony from trying criminal cases against British officials, requiring that officials accused of crimes be transported to England or another colony for trial; and the fourth required the residents of Massachusetts to house and feed any British troops sent to the colony. This last law was later clarified to specify that the soldiers be housed in the colonists' homes.

Two months later, Rhode Island called on the other colonies to send representatives to assemble the first Continental Congress, the first step toward declaring independence from England.

The American Revolution was not, as some have tried to portray it, an entirely

In 1773, after Parliament lifted the tax on tea in England but retained it in the colonies, the men of Boston dressed as Mohawk Indians and boarded three tea-laden British ships in the harbor.

There they held what has become known as "the Boston Tea Party," throwing the precious cargo overboard. In response, Parliament passed even harsher laws for the colonies.

white Anglo-Saxon protestant war, fought by a social elite. The original American patriots were made up of all races, colors, and creeds, from all economic strata. Of course, the names one remembers from history classes are largely the ones with English origins—Washington, Jefferson, Adams, and Franklin being the most famous of the colonial leaders. But even among the leadership there were "foreigners"—the Marquis de Lafayette from France, the Baron von Steuben from Prussia, and Thaddeus Kosciusko from Poland. Among the lower echelon of leaders and in the ranks, there was an even greater melting pot, most of whom don't get mentioned in the histories.

For example, few are aware that the first Jewish patriot of the revolution was Francis Salvador, a member of the South Carolina provincial congress, who was killed in battle in July of 1776.

Although most African Americans were slaves at the time, and therefore somewhat limited in their ability to participate in the rebellion, a great many free blacks and even some slaves fought for independence alongside whites. From the few statistics that are available, it appears that, of those men free to choose, the percentage of blacks who volunteered to fight for freedom was actually rather high. However, for the most part, they were denied enlistment in the Continental Army and restricted to service in the state militias.

Being slaves or the children of slaves, African Americans understood very well the importance of freedom, and they were willing to fight for it.

In 1775, when the colonies began to organize their separate militias, Massachusetts enlisted a great many blacks who served with distinction throughout the war. Some fought in the very first battles at Concord and Lexington. The most famous of these was Peter Salem of Framingham, who had been given his freedom so that he could enlist. He distinguished himself in those battles and at Bunker Hill as well.

It is not known precisely how many blacks served at Concord and Lexington, but the names of some have survived—Pomp Blackman, Cato Stedman, Cato Bordman, Cato Wood, Cuff Whittemore, Joshua Boylston Prince, and one slave known only as Pompy. At least one, Prince Estabrook, was killed. Like Peter Salem, Cuff Whittemore also served at Bunker Hill.

One African American, Salem Poor, was singled out after the battle of Bunker Hill

The American Revolution began in earnest with the battles of
Concord and Lexington, both in Massachusetts. Above is a depiction of Lexington. Among the members of the colonial militia

fighting for freedom and independence were a number of men of African origin, some slave and some free. Most notable were Peter Salem, Cuff Whittemore, and Prince Estabrook.

for distinguished service. The petition to the General Court of Massachusetts for commendation was signed by fourteen officers, and it stated that Poor "behaved like an experienced officer as well as an excellent soldier." Poor later served at Valley Forge and at White Plains.

Although most of these named were in the Massachusetts militia, other colonies included African Americans in their state troops—notably New York, Virginia, Rhode Island, New Hampshire, and Connecticut.

Because the American Revolution was itself of such historical significance, the part that slaves and slavery played in the events of the time is often overlooked. It was during the Revolution, not later in the expansionist era, that the question of the morality of slavery first became an issue of major debate among the states. Views were divided largely between those who believed in human rights and those more concerned with economic self-interest. Although most of the latter were in southern states, the division was not strictly along sectional lines, for all states still permitted slavery.

The big question for the idealists then was, as it would be for the next eighty-five years: how to end the institution of slavery with the least harm to everyone concerned?

Even before he penned the Declaration of Independence, Thomas Jefferson was proposing reimbursing slave owners for their "property" and returning the freed slaves to a colony in Africa. Being a slaveholder himself, Jefferson understood both the evils of the institution and the problems of ending it.

Benjamin Franklin was another of the founding fathers who attempted to grapple with the problem. In 1775, he and Benjamin Rush formed the first abolition society, clearly hoping to be able to end slavery along with the British ties.

In 1776, when Thomas Jefferson, aided by John Adams and Benjamin Franklin, authored the Declaration of Independence, he attempted to include a clause that would at least plant the seed for ending slavery once the colonies got their freedom. In the original draft that Jefferson presented to the Continental Congress, one of the complaints he made against the British king was as follows:

> he has waged cruel war against human nature itself, violating its most sacred rights of life & liberty in the persons of a distant people who never offended him, captivating & carrying them into slavery in another hemisphere, or

> to incur miserable death in their transportation thither, this piratical warfare, the opprobrium of infidel powers, is the warfare of the CHRISTIAN king of Great Britain, determined to keep open a market where MEN should be bought and sold and he has prostituted his negative for suppressing every legislative attempt to prohibit or to restrain this execrable commerce....

Unfortunately some of the delegates from the southern states were unwilling to sign the declaration with this clause. Finally, faced with the prospect of not having a Declaration of Independence, Jefferson, Adams, and Franklin had to accept its removal. Faced with having a Declaration without the slavery clause or no united effort against the British at all, pragmatism won out.

The matter of slavery was one of the points that most divided the members of the Continental Congress throughout the Revolutionary War. Only a few of the southern delegates stood staunchly to continue the institution, but they were enough to force the remainder of the congress to compromise on a number of occasions, the most serious being the passage of an act prohibiting blacks from serving in the Continental Army. As is generally the case in a conflict between ideals and economics, the resulting compromise leans in favor of economics.

The first time a proposal to bar blacks was brought up in the Continental Congress it was by a delegate from South Carolina, Edward Rutledge, in September of 1775. Some officers were already excluding blacks from their ranks, but it was not official, and George Washington had issued firm orders to reenlist any negroes who had been dropped and to continue to enlist any negroes who volunteered.

However, early in 1776, Washington was overruled by congress: blacks who were already serving could remain in the army, but no more could be enlisted.

The British saw this as having considerable propaganda value. They let it be known that blacks would be welcome in their ranks, and where possible they encouraged slaves to run away and cross over into their lines. Many did, and as a result there were African Americans serving on both sides in the Revolution.

This was one of the factors that eventually led congress to change its mind; the other was that many slave owners were changing their minds (because of economic self-interest). As commander in chief, George Washington wanted every able-bodied recruit he could get, regardless of color. When he instituted the policy of substitution, permitting slaveholders to send a slave to war in place of themselves, the idea of arming blacks to fight for independence was no longer so unappealing. By 1779, every state except South Carolina and Georgia permitted black enlistment.

It was also during the Revolution that some states in the North began to move toward ending slavery altogether. The first attempt to abolish slavery was made by the Massachusetts legislature in 1777, but John Adams persuaded the legislators to table the bill; with the war going on, he did not want to risk upsetting the southern states.

However, in July of that year, Vermont, which was not yet officially a part of the Union, adopted a constitution with a provision outlawing slavery. And the war was still going on when the first of the original states, Pennsylvania, abolished slavery in 1780.

When slavery was finally ended in Massachusetts in 1783, it was not by an act of the legislature but by the state's judiciary, interpreting a phrase in the 1780

Massachusetts state constitution that "all men are born free and equal" to include blacks as well as whites. The decision came out of a civil suit filed by Nathaniel Jemison against a neighboring farmer, John Caldwell, for hiring Jemison's runaway slave, Quok Walker.

After the Treaty of Paris on September 3, 1783, other northern states gradually began to abolish slavery, beginning with Connecticut and Rhode Island in 1784. New York followed in 1785 and New Jersey in 1786.

The long war ended over thirteen years after the death of Crispus Attucks in the Boston Massacre. Although the colonies had won their independence, and although countless African Americans had fought for that victory, they had not won freedom for all Americans. Most of those who fought and survived had gained their own freedom, but the majority of African Americans remained in slavery.

By the time the Bill of Rights was ratified as the first ten amendments to the United States Constitution in 1792, the country was divided between North and South, anti-slavery and pro-slavery, and it would take almost another seventy-five years to extend those rights to all Americans "regardless of race, color, or previous condition of servitude," with the adoption of the Thirteenth, Fourteenth, and Fifteenth amendments to the Constitution.

From the time that Crispus Attucks stood up to the British soldiers in King Street in Boston and died a martyr to freedom, it would take ninety-seven years for all of his race to be free and another hundred for them to enjoy fully the fruits of freedom. Yet what his country failed to do is not as significant as what he did.

He is one of the most important figures in African-American history, not for what he did for his own race but for what he did for all oppressed people everywhere. He is a reminder that the African-American heritage is not only African but American and it is a heritage that begins with the beginning of America.

Index

205

Picture Credits

Author collection: 8, 51, 52-53, 59, 64, 69, 87, 93, 95, 132-133, 149, 155, 158-159, 164, 167, 171, 173, 175, 179, 184; Boston Daily Globe: 12-13; Harper's Weekly: 72-73, 75, 126-127, 129, 151, 188-189; Library of Congress: 33; National Portrait Gallery, London: 90-91; New York Historical Society: 161; New York Public Library: 142-143, 146, 192-193; New York Public Library, Stokes Collection: 104-105, 108-109; Schomburg Center for Research in Black Culture, New York Public Library, 48; Players International Archives: 17, 25, 28, 38-39, 45; Royal Ontario Museum, Ontario, Canada: 80; Victoria and Albert Museum, London: 100.